There's Always Tomorrow

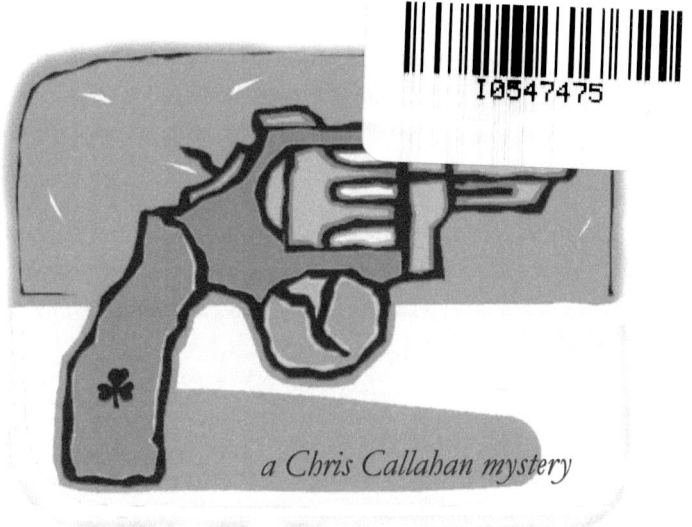

I0547475

a Chris Callahan mystery

D.G. Stern

NEPTUNE PRESS

NEPTUNE PRESS

WWW.NEPTUNEPRESS.ORG

First edition: 2012
Printed in the U.S.A.

Publisher's Cataloging-In-Publication Data

Stern, D.G.
There's always tomorrow / D.G. Stern — 1st ed.
211 p.; cm — (A Chris Callahan mystery)
ISBN: 978-0-9828098-6-0
1. Fugitives from justice--United States--Fiction.
2. Detectives--United States--Fiction.
3. Detective and mystery stories, American. I. Title.
PS3619.T477 T54 2011
813/.6   *2011907180*

Tomorrow, and tomorrow, and tomorrow,
Creeps in this petty pace from day to day…

— *Macbeth Act 5, Scene 5*—

CHAPTER ONE

There is obviously something wrong with me since cold, damp, gray days with just a trace of dirty snow actually don't depress me. It's probably just that I'm getting older and I know that soon it will be spring and that winter is just nature's way of letting you charge up your batteries.

Life is good. Pitchers and catchers will be reporting to spring training in only three weeks. I'm psyched. The Red Sox look like they've got another good team, although I am not convinced the rotation is strong enough, but they don't pay me the big bucks to have a worthwhile opinion. It's just I've been watching the Sox since Nixon was president. In good times and bad times and until recently...mostly bad times. Maybe a trip to the gym will work some of the stiffness out of my joints, one of many bad aspects of getting older, especially on cold days. I love going to the gym, especially in the late morning when everyone in attendance will either be bored housewives trying to look ten years younger or unemployed and usually overweight insurance salesmen, trying to pick up bored housewives. I'd say those are pretty good odds, especially if you're in good shape — 6' 2" and 210 pounds, which ain't bad for a guy who will be 40 in a couple of months. At least I'm employed. Well somewhat employed, since self-employed counts.

Guess I'd better fill the old gym bag and remember not to forget a change of clothes just in case I get lucky. I'm being a little optimistic, but half the battle is your attitude. I wouldn't have it any other way.

The phone rings. "Shit!" I say to no one in particular, since there's no one around. However, it never rings at this time of day unless it's a telemarketer trying to sell me something totally useless, made in China, more likely than not, and costs more than the monthly wages of the person who made it.

"Callahan."

"Got a few minutes?" The voice on the other end of the phone line is easily recognizable. It's my former boss, Captain Kendall Grover Hancock III, a real Beacon Hill Yankee in the Boston Police Department. He's smart, tough, well respected and terribly rich and he loves his job.

"What's up Captain?" I don't want to sound too curious, but a call from the boss, even the former boss, in the middle of the morning is intriguing.

"An old case of yours...one of your many cold ones, just got hot." I think I've been insulted, but I'm not sure.

"Out with the details, sir." Even after all our years together, I can't break myself of formally addressing Captain Hancock. He's earned that right.

"I'll buy you lunch and fill you in, that is, unless you're up to your thick neck in cases. Work, not booze." He can be a little hurting, but not without some justification. The truth can hurt a little.

"Your sarcasm is entirely uncalled for, especially since you called me, not the other way around."

"Touché! But I think this is something that can neither

wait nor be taken lightly. Locke-Ober at 1:30 and don't forget to wear a tie, if you even have one."

"You cut too deep," I reply. "I do actually own a tie. The one you gave me for Christmas three years ago. I think I even know where it is."

"As I recall, I gave it to you after you showed up at the Symphony as my guest wearing jeans and a turtleneck." I forgot to mention that the Captain also has a good sense of humor...more or less.

"I was heading out to the gym when you called, so 1:30 is perfect. You won't have any problem recognizing me. I'll be the one wearing a crimson tie with yellow stripes."

"Chris, this is serious stuff. I am very concerned that this is only the tip of the iceberg," the Captain slowly begins. "I want you to come prepared."

I've gotten out of the habit of carrying a weapon, especially when I'm not on assignment. Guns have an aura. If you use a gun every day, you seem naked without it. If you get used to going naked, figuratively not literally, carrying is awkward and whenever I do carry, bad things happen...like someone gets killed. I guess if it's not me, it's okay, but still in all, guns have a way of getting you hurt. Maybe that's why I only lasted twelve years on the force, nine in homicide working for the Captain. "Captain, what the hell is going on?"

"Carmen Ciccio was found dead this morning. Two shots were pumped into the back of his head at close range." His voice is flat, matter of fact.

"That was only a matter of time," I reply. This guy being shot does not rise to the level of an iceberg or even lunch at Locke-Ober's.

"Maybe, but his body was found propped up on the front stoop of Mickey's."

"Christ! Mickey's one of ours...yours. Think it's a calling card?"

"I don't know. That's why we need to talk." Captain Hancock never reveals his inner self when he talks, but I sense heightened apprehension.

"Did anything happen to him...or Eva?"

"They've been moved to a safe place. See you in one hour and forty minutes. Better exercise quickly and stay away from the married ones."

"Got it, boss." I hang up the phone.

I live in Cambridge so I have transportation options. Mostly I have parking options. I prefer to drive if I can find a parking space within a reasonable distance of my destination, but going into Boston during the week dictates riding the Red Line, a part of Boston's infamous subway system that connects Harvard Square with the financial district.

Lunch at Locke-Ober requires a couple of additions to my wardrobe. I quickly return to my bedroom. It's really not too much of a mess — sort of. I should break down and hire a cleaning lady...person.

I grab the Captain's gift tie (I actually own several) and blue blazer from my closet, pick up my gym bag, set the alarm and head off. I live right across from what was Radcliffe College until it merged with Harvard. It was better when it was only girls...women, even if they all were smarter than I, a mere Boston College graduate. Twenty minutes ago, I was thinking about baseball, and now I have to deal with the fact that my former best friend is on the receiving end of a very serious message. I forgot to mention that Mickey is shacking up with my former wife. I guess that sounds petty. Petty or not, I'm still pissed. The only good thing is that Eva and I didn't have kids. That would have been a total disaster.

Even the thought of going to the gym and seeing all those trim figures poured into work-out tights seems somehow less appealing than before the Captain's call, but the opportunity to view a few well-sculpted bottoms remains sufficient incentive to get my own butt in gear. Besides, lunch at Locke-Ober requires a big time appetite. Dining out is one of the things upon which the boss spends his not insignificant inherited fortune. He drives a carpool vehicle when he's not walking, wears understated suits, albeit from Brooks Brothers, always accented with a silk pocket handkerchief, and lives in the family brownstone off Beacon Street, with a small staff. Other than the fact that he graduated from both Harvard College and Yale Law School, he's just one of the guys and the reason he's done so well on the force is that he has never asked anyone to do anything he's not prepared to do himself and he is loyal to his people, especially when they are down.

When I got shot, Eva decided that Mickey had a better future on the force than I did. Guess that's the difference between riding a desk and riding a patrol car. Fuckin' Mickey. He was my friend, my best friend. When I asked him to look after Eva until I got back on my feet, I didn't mean he should sleep with her. You just don't do that. I shouldn't lay all the blame on him. Eva is a survivor and has a way of getting on with life. Until today, I hadn't really given her any thought in over six months. It's a big improvement.

The Captain was always there for me. Actually, everyone in the Department was supportive. I know Mickey has taken a lot of shit from the guys, but he fuckin' deserved it. I guess because it could have happened to anyone. I was just lucky that the bullet hit me in the backside. However, three more inches up and it would have hit my spine. I didn't like the odds. The Captain and I spent a lot of time talking about the future. He thought that going private would keep me active...and safe. I get a lot of referrals from the boys in blue and whenever I uncover something to share, I do. One hand washes the other.

That was then and today is today.

CHAPTER TWO

The ride on the T (short for MBTA-Massachusetts Bay Transit Authority and formerly MTA of Charlie and Kingston Trio fame) from Harvard Square to Park Square takes less than fifteen minutes at mid-day. My daily commute consists of walking from one room to another.

Although it's only about a five minute walk from the top of Boston Common to Locke-Ober, the full spectrum of humankind is on display. I pass scores of homeless men and women whose entire worldly possessions barely fill the shopping bags they cling to for protection. Less than a block away, a beautiful woman alights from a pale gray Bentley to enter the Parker House for lunch or maybe a dalliance. The contrast between her life and those whose lives are spent on the edge is not lost on me. Being a cop will do that. I've been fortunate not to have been burdened with either extreme. Being in the middle is perfect for me — a middle-aged Irish kid from Southie. However, I have to deal with the here and now and my shoulder holster rubbing against my body reminds me why I'm here. Which is...what?

One does not open the door at Locke-Ober, it is opened for you by a wizened maitre d' named Carl. His job, some forty years ago, was to keep riff-raff out, namely women. Now, I think his mission is to ensure that each guest is wearing proper attire. Passing inspection, I am admitted. It must be the tie the Captain gave me.

"Chris, I'd like you to meet Commander Joe Marshall from the State Police." Captain Hancock's ensemble features a blue bow tie with little pink squash racquets. He may be a cop, but he certainly fits into the upper crust crowd. Commander Marshall is a whole different ballgame. He's about the size of a redwood tree and black as ebony. He extends his hand.

"I've heard a lot about you," he says, dwarfing my hand in his.

"If it's good, it's undoubtedly true. If not, it's probably a lie and anyway, I'll deny it under oath," making light of the fact that my hand is still firmly held in his grip.

"Gentlemen, your table is ready," Carl announces. He leads us into the Grill Room, which features a brass railed mahogany bar about fifty feet long. As we walk the length of the room, I wonder how many deals have been made, fortunes won and lost, all within these walls.

We follow our guide to a table at the far end of the room, with a view that overlooks absolutely nothing. Locke-Ober is located in an alley. It has neither a water nor a park view...just an alley view. Each chair is pulled out ever so slightly for ease of entry. We are each handed a huge, leather-bound menu. Carl places the wine list in front of the Captain.

A bit early by my standards, but this is the place where the three martini lunch was invented.

We are seated for all of about five seconds before the Captain starts. "Before you ask any questions Chris, I want to explain to you why I've asked you here. The State Police and our Department are cooperating in a joint effort."

"Actually, a joint problem," Commander Marshall adds...certainly not for clarity's sake.

"Here's the long and short of it. You know more about what's going down on the street than anyone else."

"Knew!" I interrupt.

"There is a certain...shall I say, urgency to this problem." The Captain is unfazed by my comment. He clears his throat. "Chris, we've gotten ourselves into a mess, a very sensitive mess, and it may be necessary to take a few shortcuts in order to straighten everything out. Shortcuts are easier for you than for us."

I wonder if that's the collective us.

"You've got certain resources that aren't available to the Department." I think the Captain is under the impression that he's making sense to me.

He's not.

"Sir, I don't have the foggiest idea what the hell you are talking about. Can we start somewhere closer to the beginning than the end?"

"Sorry, this whole thing has become a nightmare. Remember Fast Eddie Giglio?"

"Of course, he tried to kill me...twice. He wasn't very good at his job." Eddie was a second or third-tier enforcer. He did errands for some wise guys. Thank God he was such a terrible shot. "I thought the Feds had put him away?"

"Not exactly," Commander Marshall interjects.

"What do you mean, not exactly? Gentlemen, you're talking, I'm listening, but you're not saying anything."

"Eddie agreed to rat on some of his former employers and he was placed into the witness protection program until he showed up in front of the St. Louis Federal Building three days ago with a couple of bullets in the back of his head." It sounds like the collective us has now been expanded to include the Feds. Shit, that's not good.

"Do you think it's the same shooter that got Carmen? Captain, I don't see where I fit in."

"Let's order first." The Captain raises a finger, not his hand but a finger, and within a nanosecond, our waiter appears.

"Sir?"

"I'll have a bowl of lobster bisque, Caesar salad and a small pot of coffee." It's pretty obvious that Captain Hancock is a regular. He didn't even open the menu.

"Same for me, except I'd like an iced tea...unsweetened," I respond.

"Clam chowder and pork chop with mashed potato and green beans." The huge State policeman closes his menu. I guess he needs to keep those fires fueled.

So far, neither Carmen nor Eddie warrant a fancy lunch. "What are you not telling me?"

"Billy O'Brien was released from Cedar Junction a week ago." The Captain's voice is entirely too calm for this bit of news.

"What?" I almost shout. "How? Double murder one. He's only served like eight months?" The reason I'm upset is the fact that first: Billy was a childhood friend of mine — almost a brother. Second: he turned into a cold-blooded killer. And third: I put him away.

"It was an administrative error. Apparently the wrong Billy O'Brien was released." Commander Marshall is trying to sound reassuring. He fails.

"Bullshit! You put a serious killer like Billy on the street by mistake and then call me. If you're trying to get my attention, you've succeeded. If you're trying to get me to help you with this problem, you're out of your friggin' mind! Sir."

"Chris, Carmen and Eddie may have been killed by the same person. Identical MOs. We do know that they were both killed by the same gun."

I hope the waiter gets here with our soup so that I can throw it at my lunch mates.

"Captain, most high-end hit men dump the weapon after the job. It's sloppy to use the same gun twice even a thousand miles apart. What aren't you telling me?" I reach for the breadbasket, take out a still warm roll, place it on my bread plate, slather the roll with real unwrapped butter and take a huge bite, resisting the temptation to throw the remaining portion at my host. Better.

"Unless the shooter wants us to know he did both hits," Commander Marshall suggests.

After finishing the roll, I ask, "Are you telling me that, not only did an administrative mistake release Billy from prison where he was serving not one but two life sentences without parole, but that he's back on the Mob's payroll and is responsible for Eddie and Carmen?"

"Gentlemen, your soup." The waiter's face reflects no reaction to anything. I think that it's a criterion for employment at Locke-Ober. Hear, see and speak...nothing.

"More or less." Captain Hancock dips his spoon into his soup bowl. The Captain is either being circumspect or he doesn't know what the fuck is going on. I vote for the former, but hope for the latter.

I try to enjoy what is most likely the best lobster bisque anywhere. The secret I've been told is that some of the lobster shell is finely ground and added to the bisque for a special flavor.

The tureens are removed and the Captain continues. "We've got to find Billy and get him off the streets."

No shit.

"Billy may not be working for anybody at all. He may be in vendetta. We have reason to believe he's after Mickey and that obviously puts Eva in the line of fire. More likely than not, he's probably after you, too."

"Hold on Captain. This is bullshit, and you know it. There's no reason for Billy to be going after Mickey, even though he stole my wife from me. And assume you're right, what am I supposed to do about it? And why?"

"Chris."

"Don't Chris me. This is dumb. I can understand Billy coming after me...maybe, but with Billy it's strictly business, nothing personal. I think that's how he approached my busting him — strictly business — nothing personal. Which means, I'm not on his vendetta list." However, with Billy nothing is certain, although I was surprised at how easy it was to apprehend him.

I look first at Commander Marshall and then at Captain Hancock. "You both know this has nothing to do with me, so other than the heads up that Billy is on the street, what am I doing here?" I'm being set up by a man I've trusted for years and I don't like it. I don't play chess very well, but I know when a pawn is being sacrificed to save the queen.

"This has everything to do with you."

"Captain, the bisque was good, but Billy is not on my dance card."

"We need to get O'Brien. We need to draw him out into the open." The Captain's voice sounds like it's about to break. "And we need to do it immediately."

"Let me see if I've got this right. Your idea is to use me to get to Billy, which assumes you can get Billy before he gets me. Am I missing anything?" Nothing is computing.

"Mr. Callahan...may I call you Chris?" Commander

Marshall is being way too polite. "Unfortunately, you are at risk...with us or without us. And we think that we can protect you, your friend and your former wife."

"Make that former friend and former wife and I don't agree that I need protection from Billy at all."

"Gentlemen, your salads...and entrée." The waiter's timing is impeccable. Annoying, but impeccable.

I want to know why some state cop thinks I'm in danger. I don't think I am a part of this problem at all. If he thinks I'm going to stick out my neck for Mickey and Eva, he doesn't know me at all.

I nibble at my Caesar salad, which is another Locke-Ober specialty. Want to know how to tell if the Caesar salad is really homemade? Ask for extra anchovies on the side. If the dressing is homemade the restaurant will have anchovies in the kitchen and gladly serve you a side portion. If it's bottled, the restaurant won't have any. Locke-Ober uses only white anchovies — great taste — less fishy.

After a few minutes of eating and thinking, I've concluded nothing good can possibly come of this. Why do I feel like this may be my last supper? I think I'll order dessert.

The Indian pudding at Locke-Ober is on the other hand — to die for. It represents the ultimate comfort food and feeling comfortable is something I need about now.

"Chris, you okay?" The Captain seems a bit solicitous, but I guess that's his nature.

"Sorry, Captain, I was drifting. Just thinking about Billy when we were young."

"Joe, I think we should go over all the details with Chris. Everything!" Captain Hancock turns in his chair to face the giant state policeman.

"Are you sure?" he replies.

"It's everything or nothing." The Captain's voice is icy cold.

Way to go Captain.

"I guess we really don't have any choice." Neither man is giving me much confidence nor are they adding anything to my knowledge base, but if they want me to play in their game, I need to know all the rules and the players.

"Instead of going back to headquarters, let's walk to my home. I've got a very workable office and all the files are there anyway," the Captain suggests.

I hope they both realize that I am aware this entire scenario has been carefully choreographed in advance. If I'm going to be led to slaughter, I don't want to go stupid. I nod politely and rise from the table.

CHAPTER THREE

The walk to the Captain's house wends through Boston — not glitzy Boston, but real downtown Boston, facing all the same problems other older urban areas face. We leave the restaurant by traveling up an alley — I wasn't kidding about Locke-Ober being at the end of an alley — past a rather down-trodden section of empty store fronts, windows of places that either never made it, or even worse, those that were in business for a century before the economy failed to support their offerings.

We cross Tremont Street at Park and into the Boston Common. I spent a lot of my youth here...along with Billy.

Originally intended to provide a public pasture for grazing sheep, goats and cows of colonial residents, the Common, together with the Public Garden, not to be confused with Boston Garden, the home of the Celtics and Bruins, forms a truly green oasis in an otherwise concrete jungle.

Since the Commons and Garden only comprise about 75 acres in total, I subliminally hear the jeer of New Yorkers when comparing our open space to their Central Park, but if you think about the fact that the land was set aside as an open space only 14 years after the Pilgrims landed at Plymouth Rock, it evidences that Boston truly is the originator of the green movement.

The Common and Public Garden is something unique, especially to kids. It's a place where your parents took you after church. Maybe you'd get to ride in a swan boat or get something to eat from a street vendor. When you got older, it was a place to play baseball in the summer or skate in the winter with friends...friends like Billy.

I could never figure it out. Everything about Billy's background pointed to a reasonably successful life. Billy's parents were basic South Boston middle class. His dad and uncle owned a hardware store that, despite the growth of malls and discount chains, did very well. Local contractors knew they were getting quality at a fair price coupled with O'Brien service. Billy's mother wasn't the smothering stay-at-home mom. She was the nurse at St. Luke's grammar school, which we all attended.

South Boston was that way. Everyone went to the same school, the same church and played with the same kids. They say that a lot is changing with gentrification, a word I hate to use because I don't think there was anything wrong with where and how we grew up. But there must have been in Billy's case.

Billy's older sister, who doted over him, was tall, dark haired and a very talented violinist. She attended Berkeley School of Music on a scholarship and now plays for a philharmonic symphony in the Midwest — St. Louis, I think. The O'Briens lived in a two-family on P Street, but so did we. In fact almost everyone lived in a two-family. Like us, Billy's grandparents lived upstairs. They seemed nice, but to a kid, all grandparents seemed nice.

CHAPTER FOUR

I remember the first time I saw Billy lose it. I mean get so mad he turned red in the face. We were supposed to play a baseball game on the Common, against a team from Charlestown.

"Townies" were always a problem. Some schools wouldn't even play against them. Anyway, we had a kind of informal league. This was before everything was organized for kids by grownups. The words soccer mom did not mean anything to us. It was a perfect early spring afternoon. Billy and I had grabbed the Red Line from Andrews Square and gotten off at Park Street. Billy's mom was going to come to the game after she finished some errands. My parents were both working late that day. My dad worked for the City of Boston as a fire inspector, making sure that buildings complied with the fire codes. Mom worked part time for an accountant and spring meant tax time for her.

So we get there and meet some of the other kids on our team and start to warm up, you know, stretching, running and finally throwing. The "Townies" are taking batting practice. One big kid with an even bigger mouth intentionally hits the ball at us instead of hitting it out toward his teammates in the field.

After about the third or fourth time, Billy simply picks up the ball and throws it at the big kid. He throws it real hard and with incredible accuracy. It hits the guy right in the chest and you can hear the sound clear across the Common. The Townie takes off after Billy, bat in hand. Billy doesn't move. Everybody thinks he's going to get whacked real bad.

Instead he says, "Need a bat for protection, pretty boy?"

The Townie stops, looks at the bat, throws it down and starts charging toward Billy like a mad bull. Billy still doesn't move. The kid is within five feet of Billy when Billy throws another baseball, which none of us had seen him pick up, right at the other kid's face. Breaks his nose — could have killed him, especially at that distance. Blood's everywhere but the only sound is the Townie screaming in pain.

Billy walks over to the boy on the ground, spits on him, walks over to the bat, picks it up and says, "It's our turn for batting practice." Billy was only ten. It didn't get better.

When was it I realized Billy and I were so much more dissimilar than we were similar? I think we were 15. The stolen car. I guess that's the last time I considered Billy O'Brien my friend. In retrospect, even thinking a joy ride in a stolen car is a good idea, was stupid. At least I had enough sense to make up an excuse so I didn't have to go with Billy by telling him that I had to help my grandmother rearrange furniture. We all had to do things like that and Grandpa was way too old to move anything heavier than a Scotch bottle.

I don't remember how I heard about the accident. I think it was the next day on the way to school. Anyway, it seemed like Billy decided he wants to cruise the neighborhood...in a car.

Being 15 meant he didn't have a license and I'm not sure he'd even been behind the wheel of a car before, but that did not deter Billy. He picked out a car he liked and stole it. However, he didn't steal just anybody's car, not Billy boy. He steals Father Donovan's pride and joy, a maroon 1970 Cadillac Deville. That was going too far. He hadn't driven two blocks when a neighbor sees the car speed by and calls the cops. Well, they start to chase Billy, who doesn't panic. He simply goes faster. After bouncing off a few parked cars he crashes the Caddy into a convenience store down Broadway. A little girl is hurt from flying glass but somehow, no one gets killed.

Billy is classified a JD (juvenile delinquent) and spends the next three years at the state facility for 'problem boys'. Needless to say, I go off to college and Billy goes off to a life in crime, mostly petty stuff. By the time I graduate from the police academy, Billy had graduated into being a real 'bad dude'. Serious bad.

CHAPTER FIVE

"Chris, look out!" Captain Hancock's voice brings me back to the here-and-now and the realization that I almost got run down by a couple of kids on skateboards, their long blond hair blowing in the wind.

"Shit, that was close," the giant police Commander says.

I shrug. "I was somewhere else, I guess." Billy O'Brien may have been my friend, but he is a professional killer and that is reality. He'd kill me, I'm certain of that, but not to get even, and only if it's absolutely necessary. Why do I have to keep convincing myself? So, I ask myself, why does the Captain think I'll be good bait? There's something else going on...but what?

Brakes have a certain way of screeching in Boston. It's probably because they are always applied at the last minute. They do have a way of getting your attention.

"Chris, are you trying to get yourself killed?"

"Shit!"

"Didn't your mother ever tell you to look both ways before you cross the street, especially Beacon Street?"

If thinking about Billy O'Brien almost gets me run down by a car, what's it going to be like when we meet?

I can't decide if I want to meet him...period. Something keeps nagging me.

"I'm daydreaming again. Sorry Captain." Both men slowly shake their heads. Space cadet they're probably thinking. It's hard to disagree. I instinctively touch the area under my arm. Carrying a weapon can give you a false sense of security.

If someone wants you dead...you're probably going to die. Despite the fact that I am sweating, I feel chilled. God willing, it's not a premonition of the future.

The good news is that maybe I'll learn something useful from our discussions. The bad news is that probably I'm not going to like what I hear. At least we'll be in the comfort of the Hancocks' Joy Street brownstone rather than the crowded, smelly and noisy offices at police headquarters. And, I could use a brandy just about now. I don't care if the sun isn't over the yardarm.

I can understand why the Captain is in such good shape. Walking up Beacon Hill every day, together with a couple hours of squash, will certainly keep one firm in body, although I'm not yet sure about firm in mind. This whole problem doesn't feel right. I can't pinpoint why, but the pieces don't fit...so far.

As if by some mystical force, the oak door to the imposing brownstone swings open at the instant we reach the stoop. We are greeted by a man in his late 60s who looks like he should be on the set of Upstairs...Downstairs.

"Good afternoon, sir," he says. "I have taken the liberty of setting a fire in the drawing room." He even sounds like Upstairs...Downstairs.

We follow the diminutive man into a tastefully decorated room which immediately reminds me of the archetypal English gentleman's club — leather chairs and couch, portraits of ancestors, richly patterned Oriental carpets, a mahogany breakfront on which a fine selection of beverages is displayed and a splendid leather topped dark cherry partner's desk — piled high with files. The only concession to the 21st century is a brand new Mac laptop computer connected to an i-Pod. I've been in this room a number of times, but I'll never stop admiring its ambiance. It is both inviting and powerful. Basically it's a great place for a meeting.

"Gentlemen, a beverage?"

"I'll have a brandy, James. Thank you."

"Scotch, please." I didn't take Commander Marshall as a daytime drinker. This must be more of a mess than even I imagined.

"Single malt or blend?" James asks.

"Single malt, please. With a splash of water."

"With or without gas?"

"Sorry?" Commander Marshall is being given entirely too many choices.

"Tap or carbonated?" James quickly picks up on the apparent confusion.

"Tap is fine."

"And you sir?" James turns towards me.

"Do you have any Coke?" I don't drink during the day. I don't really drink at all anymore. Maybe a beer. Besides, drinking always puts me to sleep, which would not be cool.

"Diet or regular?"

"Regular, please...with ice." I hope I don't have to make any other decisions. I'm exhausted.

After being served, the Commander and I each take a seat in the two large leather chairs adjacent to the fireplace, while the Captain walks over to his desk.

"We don't have time to come up with a fancy plan.

Billy's out there...and close by." Captain Hancock's words don't fill me with a warm and fuzzy feeling.

"Any ideas?" Commander Marshall doesn't have a plan either.

"Maybe I should plan a long trip to some tropical clime and if Billy follows, we'll know he's after me." I don't hear any laughter.

"This is the best we've come up with." The Captain is all business, which I guess is good. "Chris, you will go from here to the bar at the Four Seasons."

"And get drunk. It's not the tropics but from personal experience, they make a mean piña colada." I know I shouldn't interrupt but it was way too tempting.

"Chris, you are closer than you realize."

Closer to what? Maybe I misread the Captain.

"You'll pick up a beautiful blonde. You'll flirt, have a few drinks, dinner and, in a move completely inconsistent with your persona, get a room and retire with the young lady."

"That's it?" I look around and note that both the Captain and Commander are serious. The hair on the back of my neck stands up. It's an instinctive reaction that has saved my ass on several occasions. But why am I reacting this way in the presence of my former boss and friend.

"Not entirely," the Captain says in a less than reassuring voice. "To be perfectly honest, Chris, we haven't had the time to get everything set up exactly the way we would otherwise prefer. Circumstances simply do not permit elaborate planning. Anyway, the dynamics are fluid and probably the best plan is no plan, except to select people who are most able to respond as circumstances unfold."

"Thanks for what I think is a compliment, however, as you will recall, there was a very good reason I retired from the force. One which I thought you understood and besides, I'm rusty."

I think I am making myself perfectly clear. This is an altogether bad idea, and dangerous.

"Chris, you are not as rusty as you think. You know O'Brien. You always adapted your tactics to the events as they evolved."

"And as I recall, people were always shooting at me."

After swirling the amber liquid in his crystal snifter, the Captain takes a long sip of brandy. "Basically, we don't have any other choices."

"Captain, that's one of the things that bothers me. Are you telling me the combined resources of the Boston Police Department, Massachusetts State Police and, it seems both the U.S. Marshal's Office and FBI, can't come up with someone more suitable than a washed-up ex-cop? I don't buy it."

"I'm not trying to sell it, Chris. It's true. There is nobody who can get as close to Billy O'Brien as you can without getting killed...or killing him. Neither of which is a desired result." The Captain rises from his desk and toward the fireplace. Funny, I don't feel any warmth coming from the blazing logs.

"Isn't killing Billy the ideal result?" It seems like a reasonable question to me. Save the taxpayers tons of money keeping Billy in prison for, say, the next thirty or forty years. I get that nagging sensation again.

"It's not that simple." Commander Marshall finally says something, although he continues to add nothing to my knowledge base.

"Sir, I want to thank you for the wonderful lunch, but I'm not your boy on this one." I place my now empty glass carefully on a coaster.

"Quite frankly, you are being less than candid and

Commander Marshall has said nothing of substance. I respect you, I like you, but my gut says that you...both of you are withholding a whole ton of information that might affect my life or that of others. Sorry." I push myself up from the chair.

"Relax, Chris," the Captain holds his hand up like a crossing guard. "I have been specifically told to keep you on a need-to-know basis, but it is clear that you need to know a whole lot more if this is going to work. I want to have a few minutes with the Commander. We need to make a couple of phone calls." The Captain reaches under his desk and within a matter of seconds James opens the drawing room door.

"Sir?"

"Would you show Mr. Callahan into the conservatory?"

I try to suppress a smile. It's like being in a real live game of Clue. I hope Colonel Mustard doesn't join me with a wrench.

"Please follow me. Would you care for some more refreshment?"

James glides through the door. I follow. To say that I have no idea what's going on is a gross understatement. Maybe I should have something stronger than a Coke. Then again...maybe not.

CHAPTER SIX

Did Einstein ever develop a theory explaining why time passes more slowly at certain times than at other times? It's a known fact that an hour can last forever or just fly by. Depends on how you are spending the time. Waiting in the Joy Street conservatory, time stands still.

The room is sensational and showcases a concert Steinway grand piano. Not many rooms can make a concert grand look small, but 14-foot ceilings create an impression of vastness. I wonder how much time the Captain devotes to practicing.

The sheet music neatly piled on the bench certainly gives the impression of being actively used. Andrew Lloyd Weber, Gershwin, Beethoven, Chopin and even Queen.

I resist the temptation to sit down and try my scales. I remember my mother saying to me when I was about eight or nine that when I grew up I would be sorry for not continuing with piano lessons. I'm not sure she was right. Truth be told, I would have been a lousy student anyway.

What red-blooded American kid will sit and practice the scales when the alternative is playing baseball? Not me!

And I couldn't fit a piano in my apartment anyway. I wonder how much longer I am supposed to hang out waiting to do something I don't want to do in the first place.

"Sir." James is really quiet, like sneaky quiet. "I brought you another Coke with ice. Captain Hancock said he should only be another five minutes. He mentioned something about being joined by a woman and two other gentlemen."

"A woman?"

"Yes sir, that is what the Captain said."

"Curiouser and curiouser," I mumble to myself.

Instinctively, I look at my watch. You know that hour I've been waiting...doing nothing? It's only been fifteen minutes.

"Thanks, James." I take the glass from the proffered platter upon which he has placed not only the Coke, but ice in a silver bowl with silver tongs for ease of service. I guess grabbing a handful would be in bad form. James thoughtfully presents another bowl, silver of course and chocked full of smoked almonds. My personal favorite. It is apparent that one's fingers are used infrequently in the Hancock household. An appropriately small silver spoon has been placed in the almond bowl. A clear indication on how the almonds are to be removed. From bowl to hand via a spoon. Seems like a waste of effort. I'll bet the Captain doesn't eat salted in the shell peanuts. Can you imagine going to a Sox game and not eating peanuts — and not dropping the shells under your seat?

James places the serving tray on a small sideboard and exits as silently as he had entered. Drinking Coke from a crystal glass takes away a little of the fun we used to have as kids when we'd look on the bottom of the Coke bottle (never a can) to see which of us had the bottle from farthest away. Those were the days of small bottling facilities, each of which would stamp the city and state of origin on the glass bottom. Usually the victor only got bragging rights until the next time we went out, but occasionally we'd all chip in and buy the winner a second Coke. Why am I thinking about Coke bottles at a time like this? Because I'm bored and getting restless. I should never have answered the damn phone.

After what seems like another hour, James announces, "Sir, would you be so kind as to follow me back to the drawing room?"

I think formality has its place, but inasmuch as the drawing room is only across the hall from the conservatory, needing a guide only adds to my sense of doom and gloom.

James opens the door and I enter. Neither Captain Hancock nor Commander Marshall looks very happy.

"Sit down, Chris," the Captain begins. "If we are going to put you in harm's way, I want you to know the gravity of the situation and the potential ramifications if this thing blows up. I have asked three people to join us: Peter Spinelli, who you may remember, Roger Feinstein, assistant United States Attorney for the District of Massachusetts, and Detective Elizabeth Browne from the State Police."

"Sir?" I am dumbstruck by the reference to Pete Spinelli. "Didn't Pete leave the Department right after I did?"

"Correct." Captain Hancock's reply was short but not enlightening. What was another ex-cop doing here?

"Chris," the Captain continues. "Peter was recruited by the CIA. He's now the Agency's number one guy in New England."

"No shit," I mumble so that no one can hear me. The Who's Who is getting less and less to my liking. U.S. Attorney's office and CIA working on the same case. This does not bode well...for me.

"Roger Feinstein is an ex-Navy SEAL who went to

Harvard Law School and is now in charge of the organized crime taskforce in Boston."

"And Detective Brown?" I thought I should ask.

"Detective Browne is very pretty and very smart." It's encouraging to hear something from Commander Marshall that I understand. "Liz has been with the state police for nine years since graduating from Northeastern Law School. She is the liaison among local, state and federal agencies for organized crime investigation. She is also a very accomplished marksman."

"Marksman?" Iask no one in particular. I wonder why he added the part about Detective Browne being a good shot? I feel outnumbered. Three lawyers together in one room.

"Captain, as I see it, a clerical error led to Billy's release. Billy didn't escape, he was set free from a state, not a federal, prison for murders with no known connection to the international spy community. Would you please explain why such an eclectic band of law enforcement agencies have banded together in the pursuit of Billy O'Brien? Captain, I'm serious, with each passing minute, this entire operation is making me increasingly uncomfortable. And my participation is becoming less and less likely. Basically, I don't have a friggin' clue what you folks have done or are considering doing in the near future."

"All will be made clear as soon as the others arrive, which I expect to be shortly. We don't have a lot of time, but I promise you that when our presentation is complete, you will not only understand the urgency of the situation, but will appreciate why you are a critical part of the solution." The Captain still hasn't reassured me at all.

"To be completely candid with you, sir." I'm not sure where I am going with this. "I don't feel comfortable and I think that before I get in any further, I should opt out. It's not my problem and while I appreciate your concern for Mickey and Eva, my connection with and to Billy O'Brien is over."

"You can't go!" Commander Marshall pushes his giant frame up from the seat. I am not intimidated, although I probably should be.

"Wanna bet?" I don't want to sound too articulate.

"Both of you sit down this instant!" Captain Hancock shouts. The Captain rarely raises his voice.

"Chris, give me one hour. That's all. If you feel the same way then, you are free to leave. No strings attached."

For the Captain, I can spend another hour, although my mind, such as it is, has decided that nothing good is going to come of the meeting.

"Fine." I nod to the still seething Commander.

Looking back at the Captain, I say, "One hour." Consciously or unconsciously, I look at my watch. It's only 3:30. A drink would be nice, but very stupid.

CHAPTER SEVEN

We only have to wait about ten minutes until the first of the threesome arrives. Wait a minute. The captain said I was closer than I realized.

Closer to what?

U.S. Attorney Roger Feinstein. Although he's only about 5' 8", his jet-black hair, bright blue eyes, chiseled features and firm handshake all reflect his SEAL training.

"Thanks you for coming on such short notice Roger," Captain Hancock says.

"I am acutely aware of how important this is." Feinstein's voice is smooth. He's probably a great litigator.

Before I have a chance to probe into what is so important, James knocks and enters the room. "Your other two guests have arrived." He beckons in Pete Spinelli, who looks a whole lot better now than he did when he left the Department. CIA types don't eat donuts and coffee, I guess. Pete is followed by a knockout — a simply gorgeous blond woman who is almost six feet tall, wearing a basic black cocktail dress, short but not too short. Wow!

"Pete, you remember Chris," the Captain begins.

"It's been a while. How are you, Chris?"

"And this is Detective Elizabeth Browne." She offers

her hand since I'm apparently standing, albeit comatose.

"I've heard a lot about you, Lieutenant Callahan." Now that's a sure-fired way to wake up a guy. Call him by his former rank. Respect or is there some other meaning?

"Good things, I hope." My reply is a bit lame, but within the bounds of professionalism.

"May I get anyone some refreshment? Cook is preparing a selection of tea sandwiches which will be up shortly," James announces glancing first at the Captain, then at Detective Browne.

"I would love some hot tea — Earl Gray, please." Liz Browne quickly replies, setting the tone for subsequent requests.

"Lemon and sugar?" James is right on the ball.

"And some honey if it's not too much trouble." Her voice has a purring quality to it. What is she doing in law enforcement?

"Coffee, James," the Captain announces. It is obvious that it will be served exactly how the Captain likes it.

"Same," Pete Spinelli follows.

"Tea...black," Roger Feinstein adds.

"May I have another Scotch?" Commander Marshall answers very quickly...like he needs the Scotch...now.

"Mr. Callahan?"

"I think I'd like tea as well. Earl Gray, please. Lemon, but no sugar. Thanks, James."

"Gentlemen...and lady, while we wait for drinks and food, I want to provide Chris with as much information as he thinks he needs, not what we think he needs. I have promised him that unless he is completely satisfied with our presentation, he may leave in an hour. We had better sound convincing or we are all going to be in deep — " The Captain pauses realizing that Detective Browne is present.

" — shit. And I agree." Liz Browne breaks the tension.

"Thank you detective. Well said." Captain Hancock nods his head toward the breath-taking Ms. Browne.

Hmmm, maybe this assignment has some real possibilities.

"Chris, I know I told you that Billy O'Brien was released from prison as a result of a clerical error. That is not entirely true. We contrived the error. Well, not exactly we." The Captain's words hit me like a ton of bricks.

"You mean you let a cold-blooded killer out on the street intentionally?" I am incredulous. Why is no one else upset?

Spinelli rises from the leather chair in which he had taken refuge. "Chris, there's an important piece of this puzzle you don't know. Billy was in the employ of the CIA when those two guys were shot." Pete starts to pace back and forth and I'm about to jump up and strangle someone. Shit! Billy...a spy?

"Look, the Agency can't operate domestically and we can't assassinate people. However sometimes things get out of hand and despite precautions, bad things happen. I'm not defending the practice, but times have changed and our country's national security needs have changed. The two who Billy may have killed were up to their necks in terrorist activities..."

"May have killed? He's serving life at Cedar Junction because he did kill them." I look around and note that nobody seems to be listening to me. The nagging feeling is back.

"Chris, please, let Peter finish." The Captain sounds like my third-grade teacher.

"The Agency didn't have enough hard evidence to arrest these guys. Actually we didn't even have enough to even get a search warrant. We needed someone to keep an eye on what they did, who they met with and where they went. Billy was our eyes and ears."

"Billy and terrorism, I don't buy it." I feel another trickle of sweat rolling down my side.

"Believe it! Not the Muslim-jihad type terrorists, but the good old-fashioned homegrown type. The far right. These guys are dissatisfied with everything that's going on in the country. Like affirmative action, President Obama, immigration policies, jobs leaving the country. American extremists, some of whom live in good old Southie. Who better than Billy to provide us with information, except something went wrong and we don't know what, how or why. As I recall, an up-and-coming young homicide lieutenant arrested O'Brien and he has been locked up tighter than a..."

Pete pauses to rephrase. "Anyway, he has been unavailable to brief us about the shooting ever since." Pete looks right through me.

"How the hell was I supposed to know? I was doing my job."

"You weren't supposed to know, Chris. You couldn't know. It was just bad timing. Two guys end up dead and Billy goes to the can. We need closure. We need to find Billy, talk to him and get a handle on what went down. We need to know what he knows about the killing. What he thinks. Who else might be involved. Basically we know... shit." Pete starts to wring his hands.

He's a heart attack waiting to happen and I still don't buy the connection between Billy O'Brien and the CIA.

"To someone like Billy, working for the CIA is giving a sociopath a license to kill!" The sound of my voice is loud even to me.

"It's worse than that," U.S. Attorney Feinstein interrupts.

"Worse? Fuck! How much worse can it get?" I forgot that Detective Browne was in the room. I look directly at her. "Sorry."

Her eyes meet mine. "As hard as it might be to accept, I've heard the word before and even have used it on occasion." This woman is something special.

"Billy also did chores for the FBI."

Before Roger Feinstein can say another word, I stand up and turn to the assemblage, "You call yourself representatives of law enforcement. You're the criminals. Captain, I don't need an hour, I'm through."

"Please, Chris. It's complicated, I know, but the pieces will fit together." Now, even the Captain doesn't sound so sure.

"Okay, you've got forty more minutes and if I'm not satisfied..."

I pause. "I was about to say that I'd report each and every one of you to the authorities, except I can't figure out who the authorities are since you are all co-conspirators. It's illegal, it's immoral, and given a few more minutes I'll come up with some more choice words." My heartbeat has doubled in the last ten seconds.

"You are jumping to conclusions Mr. Callahan," Roger Feinstein's voice booms.

Suddenly the door opens. James, followed by a woman who looks like James' twin sister, enters. "Please put everything on the breakfront." The Captain certainly hasn't lost his sense of propriety. Feinstein eases up, a little.

Nobody moves toward the food and beverages.

"I'm going to interrupt Attorney Feinstein's presentation to say that my Department had no knowledge of O'Brien's connections with either the FBI or the CIA until two days ago. The Chief of Police received a call from the Massachusetts Director of Public Safety, who is in charge of the Department of Corrections. The long and short of their discussion was that Billy O'Brien had been released from prison...by accident. Since it was our Department's bust, actually your bust, the Chief asked me to look into things. Quite frankly, he felt that a lot of BS was being thrown in his direction and he was real uncomfortable with the explanation he had been given. And he was angry that Billy was on the street again. I did some digging and Chris, I didn't like what I found." Captain Hancock looks first at Spinelli, then at Feinstein.

Okay, I'm reasonably satisfied that the BPD isn't involved, except possibly in a cover up.

"What about the State Police, Commander Marshall?" I try to maintain cool. I'm not doing a good job of it.

"The State Police also didn't have any idea that O'Brien was working for the Feds. Although O'Brien's name would come up from time to time, it was usually associated with some minor arm-twisting. You know, collection stuff for small-time hoods. Liz, do you have something to add?"

Commander Marshall is passing the ball off as soon as he can and as usual without adding anything. This guy is fucking useless.

"About a year ago, just before the two murders, I heard from a couple of people, reliable people, that O'Brien had been providing information. To whom wasn't clear. I checked around and nobody pegged him as a snitch. Quite the contrary, he appeared to be a Family man all the way. Low end stuff, but loyal. I went to Commander Marshall with this and he wasn't able to get anywhere either. So we shrugged it off." Liz walks toward the breakfront. "We didn't have an inkling that O'Brien was working with either the FBI or the CIA." She arrives at the tea service, picks up a cup, looks toward me and says, "May I serve anyone?"

CHAPTER EIGHT

I wish I had ordered a Scotch like Commander Marshall, except that I abhor Scotch. In fact, since I left the Department, I only drink beer...infrequently.

"This whole thing is still as clear as mud," I say. "Nothing makes sense. Billy O'Brien, a tough guy for the Mob, that I can understand. But an informer, even worse, an operative, for both your agencies. That makes no sense at all."

"Here goes...from the beginning," Pete Spinelli starts.

"At last," I sigh. Five pairs of eyes stare at me. I couldn't care less if everyone else in the room thinks I'm being sarcastic. I am and I have every right to be.

"After Billy was sent to the home for little wanderers for stealing the priest's car, he quickly learned a couple of real important lessons, like what he had done was real dumb; and like without an education he was a bum, and like he wasn't as tough as he thought he was. Apparently the latter took a few encounters with some very tough kids. But Billy also found out that people liked and trusted him, albeit the wrong people. He was having a hard time making the required adjustments necessary for living in the can when luckily he met up with Cletus LeDay, a counselor at the facility. Cletus saw potential in Billy. After some tough love, he convinced Billy to apply himself to academic pursuits."

"Why does that name sound so familiar?" I ask.

"Cletus LeDay was a football player at Boston English about fifteen years ago," the Captain adds. "He was a very good football player. He was also very bright. He received a full scholarship to Brown. Unfortunately, one evening in his senior year Cletus went for a ride with some not-so-bright friends, who decided that robbing an all-night diner was a cool thing to do. Although Cletus never left the car and everyone was pretty much convinced that he didn't have any idea of what was happening until after it had happened, the judge gave him an adult sentence of twelve months at MCI-Concord. Despite the fact that it was his first altercation with the law, the judge wanted to send a message to the kids in the community that crime would not be tolerated. Brown withdrew not only the scholarship, but his acceptance as well. LeDay's life was in shambles. He served four months and was released. Since he had accumulated enough credits before the incident at one of the country's most competitive high schools, he was admitted to Boston University but without financial aid so he was able to attend only part time. It took him seven years to graduate, but he did so with honors, in child psychology. He started working with the prison system and became one of the truly bright stars in working with troubled adolescents."

"Captain, how come you know so much about LeDay?" I ask.

"I arrested him and his friends. At his trial, I told the Court that he was simply in the wrong place at the wrong time. I urged the judge to cut Cletus a break, but it fell on deaf ears." Captain Hancock slowly shrugs his shoulders.

"I was able to pull some strings and get him into BU. I offered to help him with tuition, but he refused, saying that it was important that he do it himself."

"What's he doing now?" I ask.

"He's dead. Cletus never left his neighborhood. Worked with the local kids and lived with his mom in Dorchester. One night, he tried to break up a fight between a couple of gangs and once again ended up in the wrong place at the wrong time. Such a waste." I've never seen the Captain react like this before.

"Sir?" Pete Spinelli clears his throat in an I don't want to be rude, but sort of way. "May I continue?"

Captain Hancock nods and takes a sip of coffee which Liz Browne has served.

"Cletus LeDay saw that O'Brien could be an asset rather than a liability to law enforcement and convinced Billy that he could do a lot of good by being an undercover resource. Over the next three years, on one hand Billy took on the persona of a punk kid who was always going to be in trouble, while working with Cletus on developing his skills as an observer of people and events. Needless to say when he was released, Billy was immediately recruited into the world of organized crime. He was able to operate without raising any suspicions for years. He provided the FBI with invaluable information about the comings and goings of the Boston syndicate. O'Brien was a master of doing small jobs, basically roughing up thugs who the BPD would have liked to rough up — no offense Captain — without anyone thinking he was more than he appeared...a thug himself. The only break from character was that Billy enrolled, under a fictitious name, at Harvard University as an extension student. He actually received a degree...in classics."

"No shit!" I blurt out. "I thought that Billy was a no-good low life who was going to end up in the morgue."

"Pete, may I?" U.S. Attorney Feinstein is altogether too polite. "Since Billy was initially working for us, we became his handlers and ran interference when either state or local authorities got too close. Several times we had to share certain information with O'Brien so that he didn't end up arrested by you folks."

"Damn it man, are you telling me that you sabotaged our operations?" Suddenly the Captain is real hot under the collar.

"And ours?" Commander Marshall demands. The Scotch has had no affect on him.

"The Bureau determined that it was a small sacrifice to make in order to keep our information source operational," the former SEAL replies.

This is getting out of hand and as the only outsider, I finally decide to get involved. "What? Didn't you think the BPD or the State Police could be trusted? If I'd known what was going on, I would have handled these murders differently."

"That's the point." Feinstein is pushing all the wrong buttons if he wants my help. "The Bureau didn't want you to handle things differently. Look, the BPD is a great Department, but we couldn't afford any leaks. O'Brien was...is too important to us and to the CIA. He knew what he was getting into. He wanted to be a part of the solution, not a part of the problem. It's that he did things a little differently."

"Have you always had this gift of understatement?" I'm angry, but relieved. "So what's the big deal about Billy? He's on our side, whoever our is, right?"

"Well, it's not that simple." Feinstein continues. "First,

Billy was totally kept out of the loop about his release and understandably he doesn't know who to trust. If he comes to ground, his life might be worthless. If the Mob suspects anything, they will put out a contract and Billy doesn't have the resources to protect himself. If he stays underground, he's got to be worried about somebody making him or the cops grabbing him."

"There are still way too many holes in your narratives, like who killed Eddie and Carmen and why?"

"That's the rub." Pete Spinelli starts to pace again. At this rate he'll wear out the Captain's deep blue Persian carpet. "Ever since Chris arrested O'Brien, he has been incommunicado. If we had tried to talk to him in the slammer, his life would have been worthless. Consequently, we know jack shit about anything."

I didn't have to sit in meetings for the better part of a day to conclude that the CIA knows jack shit. No revelation there.

"Pete, you've already said that. What I'm asking is quite different. What's the connection between the killings of Eddie and Carmen and Billy?" My gut tells me something really significant is still missing. And why is it nobody is telling me?

"I'm sorry, Chris," Pete begins. "I forgot to tell you that it seems that Carmen, Eddie and the two men Billy appears to have shot were all killed by the same gun."

"And that's something you just forget to mention?" I wonder how much time I would serve for punching out the regional director of the CIA?

"Chris, Carmen and Eddie were about as far from terrorism as Little Orphan Annie, so the connection between the shootings is still unclear."

Two thoughts immediately come to mind. First, once

a cop, always a cop. I can't help it. Second, although Billy seems to have had the opportunity to commit all four murders, the motive is still missing.

"Has anyone checked the ballistics of the bullets used to kill Eddie and Carmen and ice the two clowns for which Billy has been serving time, with other gangland-style murders committed in the last couple of years to see if there are any matches?"

"Pete, Roger, I think that Chris has just made an excellent point about crosschecking ballistics," Captain Hancock says.

Looking rather sheepish, Pete says, "I hadn't thought about that, had you Roger?" The former SEAL shakes his head.

This is a good example of why beat cops hate desk cops.

"I think a short break for some sandwiches and some phone calls is warranted." The Captain is not pleased that both the FBI and CIA failed to implement the most basic ballistic crosscheck. He hates sloppy police work. But then again, neither the FBI nor the CIA are police.

"It's also a time to freshen up." Liz Browne, who has been rather quiet, asks, "Where is the ladies' room?"

Hopefully there's also a men's room. Two Cokes and a cup of tea and my teeth are floating or they would be if I wasn't grinding them in fury. I hate being set up and if it wasn't for the fact that I think that the Captain is also being set up, I'd simply walk out. Either our domestic and foreign intelligence services are being run by a bunch of incompetents, or information is being withheld...once again.

CHAPTER NINE

Both as she leaves the drawing room and when she re-enters, each of us follows her movements — graceful and controlled. There's absolutely nothing wrong with showing a beautiful woman a little eye attention.

Rising as she enters, I say, "I'll serve the sandwiches."

She's probably got a significant other, who would tear me into little pieces if he knew what I was thinking about his old lady. There, I'm being my good old crude self yet again. I might as well actually get the sandwiches now that I'm up.

"Snack anyone?" I whisk the tray from cop to cop. I'm actually getting a little hungry myself, even after my huge lunch. I've probably burned my quota of calories just trying to get some useful information from this group. Watching everyone watching everyone else in this group could become a full-time job. I've never been with so many people who say they are on the same side but who are so uncertain of the others.

"Captain, I still don't understand where I fit into this. So far, everything I have heard sounds more like a bad TV movie than real police work. For example, why doesn't Billy just put in a call to Pete or to his handler at the FBI?

What's the big deal? I'm sure he can find an untraceable phone somewhere." I have to admit that I haven't seen an operable pay phone in years.

After wiping the corners of his mouth with a bright red handkerchief, Captain Hancock says, "O'Brien is a real wild card. Since his arrest, he has refused to speak with anyone from the Boston PD. Same is true with the State Police. Right?"

Commander Marshall, whose second glass of Scotch is already empty, simply nods.

The Captain continues. "No one knows what happened to the two guys who were killed. Billy refused counsel at trial and has never said a word. Based on what I've heard, O'Brien might not have been the triggerman. The fact that the gun that killed both Carmen and Eddie is the same gun that killed the two that Billy is supposed to have shot is too coincidental for me. I don't believe in coincidences."

"Sir?" I interrupt. "We never recovered the murder weapon. The crime scene was searched with a fine-toothed comb. Billy's apartment was turned upside down. No gun of any kind. So either Billy must have hidden the murder weapon somewhere so safe that he could find it and use it a year later to kill Eddie and Carmen or…he didn't kill those other guys in the first place and has been in jail for something he never did."

"Correct." At least it's comforting that U.S. Attorney Feinstein is listening.

"Gentlemen," Detective Browne begins, "lest we forget, Billy did nothing to proclaim his innocence, for whatever reason."

"He couldn't," Spinelli inserted.

I'm still really upset with the thought that I might have made a judgment about Billy's guilt without a case. As the gorgeous detective said, he didn't do shit to help himself. Why should I feel bad? Why? Because he once was my best friend.

"Let's see if I've got this straight. If your ballistics search turns up a connection with the weapon used to off Eddie, Carmen and the terrorists while Billy was locked up, he's off the hook, but if the gun wasn't used while Billy was in the can, he is then still very much a suspect in all the murders. Right?" I look around hoping that someone will give me a little encouragement. "Well?"

"Chris, we need to make contact with Billy. Not confrontation, but contact so we can talk to him. We need to find out what went down. He needs to know that we'll work with him." Pete is pleading.

"You guys are all full of shit!" I shout. "Billy was put away. He never said anything to anyone. The Code of Silence or some kind of answer with only name, rank and serial number. Just who was Billy protecting?"

"That's the point. It is imperative that we make certain we know what side O'Brien has been working." When a SEAL talks like a lawyer, it sends chills down my spine.

"May I ask a simple question" Detective Browne begins. "Has it ever occurred to you that Billy O'Brien may be playing on several teams at the same time?"

You can hear a pin drop.

"At the same time?" Commander Marshall sounds incredulous.

"It's clear that he wasn't working for either us or the Boston PD and the Feds were running interference." I think I see where she is going.

"May I interrupt?" I already did, but I am being polite. "Do you really think Billy is stupid enough not to assume that at some point in time the BPD or the State Police would put the connection together?"

"But you didn't, did you? Not until the shit hit the fan."
I'm beginning to dislike Feinstein's condescending tone.

"That's not the point. It's whether Billy thought his
cover would be disclosed." I'm more confused now than
I was before I started to think about the ramifications of
Billy being on both sides. Until today I always thought he
was on the dark side, but now it seems he may have been
on the good side or maybe both.

"Bottom line, we've got to get to Billy and get answers."
Pete Spinelli starts to pace once again. Very annoying and
very distracting.

"Let's say, you get to talk with Billy and he doesn't give
you the answers you want or he gives you no answers at
all. Then what? Are you going to kill him? Pete, you were
a pretty good cop. What the fuck happened? What are you
going to say? Sometimes things get out of hand." I'm sure
they can hear me across Boston Common.

"Captain, my hour is over!" I push up from the leather
chair.

"And what do you suggest we do?" Feinstein is really
getting on my nerves.

"You mean now that you've broken so many laws that
I've lost count?" My reply drips with sarcasm.

"Time out!" Captain Hancock slaps the top of his
desk. "Chris is right. I want assurances from both the CIA
and FBI that if we are successful and can bring O'Brien to
a meeting, which will be held at a place we designate, that
you will interview him only in the presence of Commander
Marshall, myself, and Mr. Callahan."

"Captain..." Pete starts his damned pacing.

"Sit down and listen! All of you!" Captain Hancock is
on a roll. "I want those ballistic results on my desk before

we conduct any interrogation. If we find that the murder weapon was also used while O'Brien was incarcerated, the Suffolk County DA's office will move, without opposition from any of you folks, that the conviction be vacated and O'Brien set free. He may then talk to you if he chooses or he may leave if he chooses. If the results are not conclusive, O'Brien goes back to Cedar Junction. Then whatever else happens will happen through the court system."

"In the interest of national security, we can't agree until we figure out what O'Brien knows." Pete has certainly learned the CIA two-step in his brief tenure.

"We have a jurisdictional issue. If O'Brien killed those men while under the aegis of the CIA, albeit tacitly, then the entire matter becomes Federal. Also the two other murders clearly have Federal implications and I think that the U.S. Attorney's office is best able to decide how to handle the fugitive."

I usually don't dislike someone quite this fast or quite this intensely. I am pissed and when I'm pissed I talk too much. In fact, it's been said that even if I'm not pissed, I talk too much.

"Unless I'm mistaken, no one has jurisdiction over me and as far as I'm concerned you can all go to hell. Well, let me limit that to you Mr. Feinstein and you Mr. Spinelli and you may take it to the bank that your employers can also go to hell. I'm not going to provide any assistance to either of you and I hope Billy rats you out, although he probably won't. Rest assured however, that I will do so, as soon as I find the right person to rat to, which very well may be the media. You guys are as bad as the bad guys, just on the other end of the spectrum and you're a lot more dangerous because you wear the mantle of authority. And furthermore, Billy O'Brien is no fugitive. You assholes let him out of jail intentionally."

"That's not an acceptable response." The former SEAL rises and begins to walk toward me. Instinctively I stand up and reach inside my coat. One more step and I'm going to put a hole in the bastard.

"Sit down...both of you!" The Captain is on his feet, as is the giant State Police Commander. Out of the corner of my eye, I notice Detective Browne remove a baby Browning from her pocketbook. How appropriate Browne with a Browning, a very accurate, although small-bore five shot automatic. The perfect accessory for a lady on the town. I ease off, assuming she's going to shoot Feinstein, and not me. I hope that's a reasonable assumption. Sensing that he has acted way out of bounds, the assistant U.S. Attorney slowly backs up toward his chair. I really want a drink. I really need a drink.

"Let me make something perfectly clear. The Feds have acted pretty high-handed to date, and that may account for your defensive behavior, but no one and I mean no one, is going to threaten anyone else in my house...in my city. Do I make myself clear?" The Captain's eyes have bored a six-inch hole into Feinstein, whose complexion has turned from beet red to ashen gray.

I wonder if Liz would have plugged the jerk. I hope so. Maybe she doesn't have a significant other. Get your mind off the lady, Callahan, there's a lot to be done. Why am I even thinking that? I'm out of here, right? Wrong. I can't leave the Captain swinging in the wind. Same with Commander Marshall, who seems especially bothered by something and it doesn't seem to be the Scotch.

CHAPTER TEN

"OK? Where do we go from here?" I ask, addressing my question to no one in particular.

"We need to reach an agreement on dealing with Mr. O'Brien, at least until this mess is sorted out." Ms. Browne says.

"Until the ballistics report comes back, there's not much to discuss," I reply.

"Actually, while the report may be useful, it's not dispositive." I'm convinced that Feinstein likes to hear himself talk, but he's a lawyer so what else is new?

"Dispositive of what? If the report finds that the weapon was used when Billy couldn't have used it, he's home free. I thought we had agreed on that."

"For the sake of argument, I agree. We also agree, do we not, that whoever shot the so-called terrorists also shot Giglio and Ciccio, and if Billy is not cleared by ballistics, he's the prime suspect and that becomes a Federal case."

"I am not going to listen to legal dribble. Either the BPD calls the shots, figuratively speaking, or I'm history." Callahan's first rule: If you think you're being set up, you probably are.

"Let me suggest something," the fair-haired State

Police detective offers. "If Billy did kill all four, why would he risk his neck and get in touch with Chris?"

At least it's not Lieutenant Callahan any more.

"To kill him."

Thanks Pete.

"Wait a second. I think we are missing something that suggests Billy may not have had any connection to the first two murders even without the ballistics report." This may be an epiphany.

"Why do we care?" I should have shot Feinstein when I had the chance.

"If we assume Billy didn't commit the murders, getting him to talk may be easier, especially if we…if I can convince him that we think he's innocent."

"That's what the report will show." Captain Hancock responds.

"In part, that's true. We have to consider the possibility that the report won't show that the gun was used when Billy couldn't have been the shooter. We need a working assumption of his innocence if we are going to open any line of communication. Think about it, not one of you has provided any motive why Billy would kill Eddie and Carmen, much less have the opportunity." I hope everyone is listening.

"What if he needed some money and filled a couple of contracts?"

"Pete, that doesn't make any sense at all. Billy's underground. He hasn't made contact with anyone." I'm cruising now.

"Anyway, it doesn't fit his profile," Liz adds. "Billy was an arm breaker at worst, never a killer."

"And remember," I wish there was a drum roll, "we never found any sort of gun or gun paraphernalia in Billy's apartment or his car or his person."

"I must admit, I've never met a killer...well, a professional killer, who didn't have backup weapons." Pete is finally talking like a cop instead of a spy.

"So what?" Feinstein asks, adding nothing to the conversation, except to hear himself talk.

"In developing a plan, especially a plan that puts my ass, not yours, on the line, isn't it nice to know that the person you're looking for isn't a cold-blooded murderer?" It is inconceivable to me that this guy is in charge of anything.

"We need to decide on how and by whom O'Brien is to be interviewed because once the plan to make contact is implemented, I suspect things are going to move very quickly." Captain Hancock sounds like his old self. Self-assured and in command.

"What do you suggest?" Even Pete Spinelli is more willing to listen now than before his colleague's tantrum.

"I'm assuming everyone agrees that getting Billy to talk is the goal," I suggest. "That means a couple of things. First, somehow we've got to get his confidence that he'll be safe."

"Sorry for interrupting you, but that's where you come in." I was afraid the Captain would say something like that.

"That means that Billy has to control the flow. Any meeting has to be on his home turf. He's going to insist on that. He's also going to want assurances that if you...any of you, isn't satisfied, then he's in the same position as before the meeting, back on the street. Captain, I'm not happy about this. I know Billy. If he's on the good side, all will be fine. If he's on the bad side, he won't even come up for air. And if he's on both sides, I'm in a shit full of danger."

"Chris is right," Liz Browne says. "It is essential that O'Brien feels he is in control and that means cutting him a lot of slack. No jurisdictional bullshit, no nothing. Since the plan calls for me to be with Chris, my ass is also on the line."

And what a nice ass it is, I think to myself.

"Explain." Suddenly the assistant U.S. Attorney is a man of few words.

"May I?" My eyes are directed at the lovely and intuitive Ms. Browne.

"Please do," she replies.

"We won't get Billy to come out into the open until he's ready…good and ready. If he does reach out to me, I want an absolute guarantee from each and every one here, both individually and on behalf of the various organizations you represent, that no action will be taken to apprehend Billy, detain Billy, interrogate Billy or in any way interfere with Billy without his consent. And Pete, just so we understand one another and that includes killing Billy." I sound like the end of a baseball broadcast when they tell you that you shouldn't have recorded the game you have already recorded without the express written authority of the commissioner. I look around the room. Everyone nods, although I think Roger Feinstein probably has his fingers crossed behind his back.

"Boy Scouts honor?" I'm acting a bit immature but I really want them to know I'm serious. "Okay, how do you guys…and lady plan on having Billy pay me a call? If Billy is one of us and I say that with reservations, how's the other side going to feel about Billy being on the loose?"

"So far, the buzz on the street is that the folks at MCI-Concord simply screwed up big time and everybody's having a good laugh, wishing O'Brien well and jealous that they weren't the lucky ones." Finally Commander Marshall participates in the discussion.

"Isn't that going to change if Billy does try to contact

me?"

I'm not sure why Pete Spinelli has to pace when he talks. "I'm sure O'Brien will be very careful, regardless of which side he's on. I think he might welcome the opportunity to tell his side of the story."

"Let's hope so." The SEAL has spoken.

"If I'm going to walk around with a target on my back, I'm going to set the rules. I talk to Billy. If I'm convinced that he's straight, I'll set up another meeting with all of you. If the whole thing stinks, I'll say good-bye and he's gone. I don't want a tail, so don't even think of having me followed." I hope I sound convincing.

"Yes…and no." Only the Captain could say something like that.

"Sir?"

"It comes down to why Detective Browne is here. We have devised a plan that we think will be most likely to bring Billy to the surface, and she's a part of it."

"Captain, you weren't kidding about the plan you told me about earlier, were you?

A slight smile crosses his face, followed by a shrug.

"Well then, I want double assurances from the State Police that Billy's movements will not be restricted and there'll be no attempt to prevent him from doing whatever he wants."

"Except to kill you." Liz Browne's voice is as cold as ice.

"That's fair." I try to sound cheerful but she's right. I really don't know Billy anymore. "Are there any specifics to your plan that you care to share with me?"

"Yes." Good old monosyllabic Feinstein.

"Before we get into the details, I'm going to excuse myself and visit the head."

CHAPTER ELEVEN

No one notices my return to the drawing room. Maybe returning wasn't such a good idea. I should have split when I had the chance. Everyone is huddled around the Captain's huge cherry desk, no doubt hatching some plan that will get me into a lot of trouble.

"May I join you?"

"Chris, I think we've got an idea," Captain Hancock answers without glancing up. "We need to make some operational assumptions, primarily that O'Brien wants to get in touch with you."

"Sir, do you have any basis for that assumption?"

"Not really. O'Brien has made no effort to get in touch with Pete or anyone at the FBI, so you are all we have."

"That's me…last resort Callahan. Captain, there is nothing at all that even remotely suggests that Billy wants to contact me?"

"That is not entirely true."

"I thought we weren't going to play games." Now the Captain is beginning to piss me off.

"Believe me, it's no game. We have nothing concrete or remotely reliable. It's just that your name was mentioned in connection with O'Brien in a conversation reported to us by an informant. He was not even able to identify the speakers, but he thought that he should tell us. He didn't know that Billy was back on the street, so I thought the comments might be relevant."

"You are not making it sound very encouraging. Sorry for blowing up."

"Chris, I admit that we are grasping at straws, but we have no choice. We need to get to Billy and soon."

"Where do we go from here?"

"Let's assume O'Brien is keeping your apartment under surveillance or at least keeping you under surveillance. It gives us the opportunity to do a start over." What the hell is the Captain talking about?

"Start over? What is a start over?" I want to remind everyone that this is not golf, no Mulligans.

"Sorry. You'll retrace your steps and return home, wait an appropriate period of time and go out again. If we're correct Billy will follow you this time, especially since it's going to be dark." There are a couple of glaring gaps in the Captain's plan, like where am I supposed to be going.

"Sir, from the top, if you please. And let's try not to omit any details that might save my life and that of Detective Browne."

"Quite simply," Feinstein intercedes, "you are to decoy O'Brien into the open."

"Stop! I've already told you that I'll talk to Billy with Liz as my cover. No one is to interfere. I mean no one at all! If Billy wants to meet with me, that's his decision and his alone. Those are the ground rules."

"He's right. Those are the ground rules." Captain Hancock is going to cover me. Thank God.

"I don't have authority!" the former SEAL shouts.

"Get it!" The Captain is hot under the collar. "You

may use the conservatory to make any calls you think are necessary, but you will get the authority or the Boston Police Department and its resources will not participate in what is becoming an increasingly unpleasant matter. I trust that you understand."

Assistant United States Attorney Feinstein nods. He's not accustomed to anyone talking to him that way. The door opens and the ubiquitous James appears.

"Please show Mr. Feinstein to the conservatory, he has some phone calls he has to make." I want to stand up and cheer, except I'm already standing and cheering would be totally inappropriate, but totally awesome. Immaturity has its place.

James beckons. Feinstein follows. Door closes.

"Thanks, boss."

"You're the one sticking your neck out, Chris. It should be on your terms, with which I agree. This isn't of our making, but we're being asked to clean it up. As far as I'm concerned..." the Captain turns toward Pete Spinelli, "I think that the Feds should kiss our behinds. Both our Department and the State Police are putting assets...real people...into a situation that has more uncertainties than I can count. Pete, I will not tolerate any surprises from our side."

"I have complete authority and have agreed to your conditions. I want you to know that I am not real comfortable with the thought that if O'Brien does make contact with Chris, but he's playing on both sides of the fence, that leaving him on the street is a great idea." I wish Pete would pace in another part of the room. He's definitely going to wear out the rug.

"If it makes you feel better, Pete, the thought that Billy was released in the first place doesn't thrill me. A couple of hours ago, I felt safe in the belief a murderer was behind bars. Now, I don't feel safe regardless of whether Billy is actually a killer or not. Having said this, maybe if I was still on the force, I might look at your problem differently. Understand that if Billy does reach out to me, and I mean if, it's because he trusts me and I cannot and will not compromise that trust." I glance around the room. Only Liz Browne reacts, albeit by nodding ever so slightly.

"If you actually have a plan, share it with me." I say after a deadly silence of about ten seconds. There's the time thing again. It seems like ten minutes.

"Let's wait until Roger returns. There's no point going over everything if his team is not on board." The Captain not only makes perfect sense, I think he's trying to make sure that the CIA is still a little unsure where we stand, although I'm not convinced that the CIA can put pressure on Feinstein's folks. This whole thing has more plots, subplots and sub-subplots than all of Steven Spielberg's movies combined. I need another cup of tea.

"Coffee...tea anyone?" I try to sound both cheerful and helpful. I'm not fooling anybody.

A light knock on the door announces James, who is returning the prodigal U.S. Attorney to us. How lucky.

"I have authority to bind the Justice Department in any arrangement we make here regarding O'Brien. We will not interfere with your attempt to meet with O'Brien, nor will the Bureau make any attempt to apprehend O'Brien for at least 24 hours after you meet." Feinstein's voice is devoid of any emotion, although I think he is seething.

"I have the feeling that you don't think Billy wants to meet with you." I still think Feinstein is holding back.

"Please understand that Justice and the CIA may not

have the same agenda. Nobody's sure why or if these murders tie together, except for the shooter."

"Actually the weapon, not the shooter." Liz Browne inserts.

Well, there's a surprise. One Fed admitting that his organization may not be on the same page as another. I think I'm going to stick real close to the Captain and of course, Ms. Browne.

"Okay, it's settled. Chris, with the help of Liz, and without any interference from anyone, will try to contact O'Brien."

"Captain, excuse me, but I want to make sure everyone understands that I'm not going to try and contact Billy, but rather I will follow your suggestions on how and where it's most likely he will contact me."

"You are correct, Chris. The plan will be for you to be accessible to Billy without excessive risk. Find out what you can and make a decision based on your discussion." The Captain is trying to give me as much wiggle room as possible, for which I am grateful.

"Can you tell me the plan now?" I'm tired of being the only one in the room who has no idea how this is going to work.

"You're going to go back to your apartment, leaving here by the back door, walking down the hill, getting on the Red Line at Charles, getting off at Harvard Square and walking to your apartment," Captain Hancock begins.

"Ah…the old start over." I really should keep my mouth shut.

"Precisely." My comment doesn't seem to affect the boss. "You will change into something more appropriate for a night out on the town and wait about thirty minutes, after which you will drive. You still have that old car, don't you?"

"Captain, are you sarcastically referring to my most trustworthy, loyal and reliable classic 1974 Chevrolet? The one I bought when I was a sophomore in college — used — twenty years ago — for $250?"

"Do you have another?" I think the Captain really likes my car, but is a little embarrassed to admit it.

"What he's driving is totally irrelevant." I really dislike Feinstein.

"True, but it's an old and private joke." I don't think the Captain likes Feinstein any more than I do. "In any event, you will drive to the Four Seasons, have your car valet-parked, go to the bar, order a drink, and then another. The bartender will be one of our plainclothes officers, but he'll have no details except that you are on a stakeout. I want to make sure that by the time you get to your third drink you'll be able to stand. Order a Grey Goose martini. It will be very smooth and cold…like fresh mountain water."

"Got it!" The thought of a real three-martini stakeout makes me laugh. I probably would be flat on my ass. "Then what?"

"You will put the moves on a very classy lady who will be sitting at the bar." Captain Hancock has a great sense of humor, but lousy timing. What the hell is he talking about? I get it…Detective Browne.

Walking over to Liz, I ask, "What's your sign?" She suddenly bursts out with a laugh that brings tears to her eyes.

"It's been a while, hasn't it?" She's trying to regain her composure.

"It's that obvious?" It has been a long time.

"Okay you two. You've got the idea. We think O'Brien will follow you and make contact in a public place." The

Captain isn't convincing me, but what the hell, it's a chance to spend some time with Liz on someone else's expense account.

"How long do we hang out at the bar?"

"If O'Brien hasn't made any contact by 11, we move into the second phase of the plan." I hate to say this or even think this, but I am losing confidence in Captain Hancock's brainstorm. I sneak a look at my watch. It's a little after 6.

"Captain, I don't want to sound less than really enthusiastic, but your plan is beginning to sound less and less like a plan at all. Why would you possibly think that Billy O'Brien would ever go into a place like the Four Seasons? Charlie's Pub...maybe, but he is not a Four Seasons kind of guy."

"It's because he's a Charlie's kind of guy. No one would recognize him in the Four Seasons. He'd be invisible." It's hard to argue with the Captain.

"Okay, so what's the second phase?"

"You'll love it, Chris." Liz Browne's smile lights up the room.

"That's not fair. You know and I don't. Fess up."

"It's quite simple. You will use your well-known Irish charms to convince this lady you just met to retire with you to one of the Four Seasons' lovely suites." Captain Hancock isn't joking. "And before you ask, a room has been set aside for your use. It's bugged."

"Let me get this straight. If Billy doesn't make contact at the bar, why do you think he'll contact me upstairs in a room?"

"More privacy." Pete Spinelli obviously is as clueless as I am.

"Chris, we've got a small window of time to pull this off. I want Billy to have every opportunity to make contact.

If nothing happens by tomorrow morning, I think the window will close." The Captain is beginning to sound ominous.

"Why do you think that there is so little time? I thought everyone is now on the same page. This might take a day or two." The thought of a couple of days at the Four Seasons with Liz makes me smile...inside. These guys all have their game faces on. No one is amused. I look at Liz who responds by raising her eyes upward. I wonder what that means.

"I have a gut feeling." The Captain looks around the room. "I'm sure that there's a contract on Billy. Nothing concrete. Joe tell him what you've come up with."

Wow, Commander Marshall is still here.

"Although our prison contacts say everything is cool, there have been little things that are bothersome."

"Like?" I'm having a gut feeling, too.

"A couple of very high end Mob hit men from New Jersey rolled into town this morning. We can't identify any other target, except Billy." Detective Browne is all professional, but the thought of being in the line of fire between some pros and Billy is making this sound less and less like a good idea. I've got to give Liz credit, she's out there too. Wait, she's getting paid to do this shit...I'm not.

"I want to get this straight." I am trying to control myself. "If Billy doesn't contact me by tomorrow morning, then you're bailing? Right? If he's so damn important, I'd think you keep after him until either you get him or somebody else gets him or he disappears. What aren't you telling me?"

"We can't take any chances," Roger Feinstein says. "O'Brien cannot be permitted to fall into the wrong hands. He knows way too much about how we operate. Way too much."

"What? Have we regressed to the assassination bullshit again?" I'm sure I woke up any ghosts who reside in the Hancock residence.

"Chris, let me explain." At this point in time, the Captain is the only one I'll listen to. "If Billy doesn't make contact, we have to assume that there is a reason."

"Like he doesn't trust any of you? Seems like a perfectly good reason to me."

"Chris, it is out of the Department's control or State Police control. By tomorrow morning, Billy O'Brien will be classified a fugitive — armed and dangerous. Maybe he'll be able to disappear, but a lot of people will be looking for him. It's not assassination but law enforcement."

"Wait! You've forgotten the ballistics report that might clear Billy. Captain, this is bullshit." My blood pressure is in the danger zone.

"Regardless of anything else, any of the crap from Justice or the CIA, Billy currently stands convicted of the crime of murder."

The Captain is right, of course.

I just don't like it. I guess if we got the wrong man or there are extenuating circumstances, Billy's the one who's got to come forward.

"Sorry about the assassination stuff. I keep getting dribs and drabs of information that you all have been thinking about for a couple of days...at least." I can't believe I am apologizing to Feinstein or to Spinelli. They're both crazy and very dangerous.

"Chris, you took my advice about protection, didn't you?"

The Captain's question makes me laugh. They've got me hustling a good-looking — a very good-looking woman, possibly spending the night with her and they're worried about protection. I get it. My gun.

I open my sport coat where I had holstered my trusty Glock 9mm. Then I lift up my right pant leg to reveal my equally trustee Colt .38 shortie tucked into an ankle holster.

"Boss, do you have any of that new light-weight body armor? Preferably, something that won't ruin the line of my sport coat? We want my performance at the Four Seasons to look genuine." My voice may sound strong, but inside I'm a wreck.

Everyone assumes that I can connect with Billy and that he wants to connect with me. What do I know about him? What does anyone know about him? Maybe he really hates me and wants to get even for being sent to jail. I don't really believe it, but denial can get you killed. I just keep remembering that Billy O'Brien was the meanest kid I ever met.

"Long sleeve or vest?" The Captain is serious. I was kidding. This is serious.

"Whatever." What else can I say?

"42 Long?" He asks. I nod. Captain Hancock picks up the phone. Suddenly he stops talking and places his hand over the receiver. "Do you use standard issue ammo or hollow?"

"Standard issue," I respond. Hollow point ammunition is no laughing matter. It can tear up a person's insides so they just bleed to death...in pain. I'm up to my neck in shit on this one.

"I'd better get going. Liz, see you at eight."

"Mr. Callahan, this is for you." James hands me a package marked U.S. Department of Defense and gestures toward a door, not the front door, but a door leading me into an ancient, but totally over-the-top room, filled with medieval knights donned in armor. I wonder if the Captain will lend me one of those swords or maybe a mace.

CHAPTER TWELVE

A chilling breeze sends a shiver through me as I walk down Charles Street. When the sun retreats into the western sky, the temperature drops quickly this time of year. Since I forgot to wear an overcoat, I'm glad for the added warmth of the single-layer, microfiber, skin-tight, bulletproof vest. At least I hope it's really bulletproof and doesn't ruin the line of my jacket.

The subway ride at 6:30 is a little slower than it was at 1:00, but all in all, it only takes me thirty minutes door to door. That means if I've got to meet Liz at 8, I've got a half hour to burn — just enough time for that beer I've been lusting after all day. If Billy O'Brien is out there watching me, I might as well turn on all the lights in my apartment to make it a little easier. What if someone is watching Billy watch me? Scary thought. Since you can bet that Billy will want to make sure I'm not carrying, I decide to ditch the Glock and hope he doesn't check my ankle.

Recalling Liz's comment about being out of practice at the dating scene, I start to panic. What should I wear? Making the moves at the gym is one thing, everyone follows the same dress code. But what about the real world? Certainly not the same thing I have on, but what?

Everything nowadays is so casual. Tie or no tie? No tie. Change into a turtleneck but keep the blazer. Forget it. That's so dated.

Wear what you're wearing. It looks good. Change the tie…just in case you run into Captain Hancock. Show him that you actually own another tie. Done. All these decisions are made while I climb up a single set of stairs to the second floor. Maybe I'll take a quick shower. Stop it! I yell at myself. I'm definitely going to drive myself crazy.

I wish I had known about Billy before I left this morning. I would have tagged the door by placing a small piece of clear tape at the bottom so that I can tell if it's been opened. It's not preventative, it is informative. Burglars… or in this case Billy O'Brien, will spend their time worrying about an alarm system. I had my system installed a couple of years ago after a rash of neighborhood break-ins. It's very good, but even a good alarm won't keep a pro out of your house, it's basically the amateur, looking for a few bucks, that it deters.

It's best to know if someone's been inside before you enter, since he…or she might still be there. I slide my Glock from its holster, click off the safety, put my key into the lock and stand back just in case someone wants to shoot me. So far so good. I slowly turn the doorknob. I hear the high-pitched sound of the system telling me it's still armed. I push the door open and stand back against the wall… again. Nothing. Since the end of the 15-second pause cycle before the alarm goes off is nearing, I decide to disarm the system. Still nothing. There is enough ambient light from the street to see that everything looks as it should. If a professional breaks into your place, he leaves it one of two ways: neat as a pin so that you never know you've had a visitor or completely trashed. The purpose of the latter is either a function of time, like how soon is the owner returning, or to send a message that you're not safe even in your own home. I quickly move around the apartment, Glock still in hand, and turn on every light. Either no one visited in my absence or the visitor was a pro, since the alarm is undisturbed.

Next stop, the kitchen. I no longer want a beer. I need a beer...then a quick shower. I am drenched in sweat. I close and lock the front door and then take a swallow from the long neck that I don't even remember taking from the refrigerator. I still haven't bought into this plan, even though it's the Captain's plan. I walk over to the living room window overlooking the street and stare at the empty sidewalk below. Here I am, Billy. The next move is yours. I strip off my shirt and put it into the laundry bag intended for the dry cleaner...next week. I peel the body armor from my soaked skin, turn on the shower and proceed to boil myself in a refreshing cascade of hot water.

After roughly toweling myself dry, I pull my new vest over my head, grab a clean pair of boxers from the dresser — nothing too gaudy. If I'm going to spend any decent amount of time with Liz Browne, I might as well know where she stands on important issues. After grabbing a pale blue Oxford cloth shirt from my closet, I begin my search in earnest for my Red Sox tie. Today's slacks and blazer will have to suffice. Sadly, I'll have to wear socks, to prevent the ankle holster from chafing. One of the things I hate most about winter is wearing socks. A pair of black Cole Haan loafers with tassels completes my killer outfit. It has been a long time.

Should I or shouldn't I have another beer? It's probably not a good idea. Must be time to fire up my trusty steed and head over to the Four Seasons. I repeat the process:

set alarm, lock door but before I descend down the stairs, I place not one, but three pieces of tape on the apartment door. I want to make sure I know whether my space has been violated when...and if I return.

The wind seems to have subsided or the combination of a hot shower and a cold beer are providing sufficient warmth that the two-block walk to my rented garage is actually pleasant. It wouldn't do to have Chris, Jr. live outside. So what? I named my car after myself. Parents name their kids after themselves.

I'm no meteorologist, but it is getting really cold outside. Maybe I should have taken a coat, but the Captain did say to valet-park the car.

I can't recall what happened first. My heart stopping or the cracking sound that sounds like the hammer of a revolver being clicked into position. I guess a bullet in the back of the head isn't a bad way to go. It's fast and painless, but at age 40...almost 40, a bit premature. I debate turning around but opt for a quick look down at my feet instead, which are standing in a small pool of water upon which a thin layer of ice had formed, now broken into a thousand pieces under my weight. Well, so much for the revolver. I quicken my pace.

What if I just scream Billy...Billy O'Brien...it's me Chris Callahan. Remember your old friend who sent you to the slammer? Want to have a chat? I really have some great ideas, although this is not one of them. Shit. I wish I had worn a coat. I'm frozen. At least the Chevy has a great heater.

A garage in Cambridge is a rarity. Street parking, when you can find a space, is always a risk, either from theft or from the rather unique way Bostonians parallel park. The typical driver will back into a space and stop only after he or she has hit the car behind. Then with equal grace, he or she will move forward until...bang, the front car is whacked. This procedure is repeated until the car has been inserted into an entirely too small space in the first place. But that's not all, parking in the winter is a real adventure. After a snow storm, owners treat their cars in one of two ways: either abandon them until the snow melts in the spring or in those rare cases when the owner needs his car and expends the effort to shovel it out, a garbage can will be placed in the parking spot to reserve it until the rightful owner returns. Heaven help the unknowing or possibly knowing, but dumb person, who parks in another's shoveled spot.

I'm lucky. Almost ten years ago, I heard that a neighbor's husband had passed away. Since she didn't drive, the garage became vacant for a really nice guy with a vintage, well aging, car. I guess it didn't hurt that the decedent was my mother's uncle. In exchange for a few chores, including snow removal, the garage is mine to use. In addition to the Chevy, I store my bicycle for those increasingly rare occasions when I decide to go on a trek along the myriad of bike paths that wend throughout eastern Massachusetts.

The good news is that the garage is not visible from the street, making a casual thief less likely to attempt to break in. The bad news is that the garage is not visible from the street, making it a perfect place to ambush an ex-cop. Shit! I wish I had installed a light with a motion detector. I just never got around to it.

I would feel more secure if I had my hand around the handle of my .38, but if I'm really going to make contact with Billy, a gun would certainly be a deterrent. At least the door opens with a clicker...a garage door opener. If I time it correctly, I can be in the Chevy, doors locked and engine running in ten seconds...fifteen tops.

I walk past my great aunt's house as inconspicuously as possible. I really don't know what else to call her. Her husband's mother was my mother's mother's sister. Growing up, we didn't see them often. Cambridge was a long way from Southie in those days...politically more than physically. Anyway, when I moved into my apartment, I introduced myself to my long-lost relatives and spent many Sunday afternoons with Uncle Patrick watching the Patriots, Celtics, Bruins or Red Sox, depending on the season. For his age, he was a really interesting guy, I thought. He'd always be better informed than I was on any subject. He read four newspapers a day, to get a balanced opinion, he used to say. Anyway, when he died, I kept visiting his wife, Ruthie, mostly to help with things she couldn't do around the house. Thus, the garage. I digress.

No one seems to be following me, although I'm not sure that's a good thing. If Billy isn't around now, how is he going to follow me to the Four Seasons? Worst case scenario is that I spend the night with the gorgeous Detective Browne. I dart into the backyard, push the garage opener, count the seconds as it creaks open, unlock the Chevy — manually, slide in, push the door lock and start the engine, which fires on the first try despite being unused for over a week. The main reason I'm never going to buy a new car is that the Chevy is fixable. It has real parts, not a computer that controls everything. I slowly back out, feeling safe inside my personal tank. At least it won't be hard to trail me into Boston. The Chevy will be the only thirty-plus-year-old car on the road. Try following a Toyota Corolla some day. Like the ad says, almost every one ever built is still on the road.

Driving through Harvard Square is always an adventure.

Between jaywalkers, lost tourists, bad drivers, inoperable stoplights and ubiquitous double parkers, you take your life in hand. Trying to get to Storrow Drive, one of the two roads that runs parallel to the Charles River heading toward Boston — Memorial Drive on the Cambridge side and Storrow Drive on the Boston side is a nightmare. Being parallel doesn't mean straight. Driving alongside the meandering river means that the Hancock Tower, a familiar local landmark, appears on your right, on your left, in front of you and finally behind you as you head into Boston.

Although the speed limit is 45 mph, traffic moves at the fastest speed physically possible based on traffic volume rather than road conditions or God forbid…safety.

There's another rather tricky part about Storrow Drive: the tunnels vary in height so much that commercial vehicles are forbidden to travel on Storrow Drive, lest they hit the bottom of the tunnel arch, which is really the top of the tunnel.

You'd figure that after all these years and all the signs announcing low clearance, there'd be no problem. Right? Wrong! Each fall, as students swarm into the area, without fail, somebody…no, some idiot, forgets and drives the basic U-Haul rental truck into a tunnel, jamming it under the granite blocks, shutting down the road and causing unbelievable havoc.

The Chevy was not made like today's nimble rice burners. It is big, solid and tends to wallow from side to side a bit, all of which explains the speed limit. What's the hurry, especially if someone is trying to follow me? Another thing, it is considered a sign of weakness if a Boston driver uses his or her turn signal before switching lanes, although it does explain road rage. Gender, here, plays no role in bad driving.

At last I reach the Arlington Street exit. Calling it an off ramp is giving it entirely too much credit. In any event, I'm dumped at the foot of the Public Garden. 'Start over' is now complete.

CHAPTER THIRTEEN

I motor along Arlington Street past the Ritz and take a left onto Boylston and slowly serpentine into the valet-parking area, which is housed under an overhang so that visitors do not have to brave the elements. Gas heaters hiss warmth, as much for the car attendants as for the patrons. It's all very egalitarian.

The Four Seasons is a classy joint and the bar is one of my favorites, although a bit pricey unless I'm working with an expense account, like following some wanderlusting husband for his jealous, but usually correct, wife. I glance at the eight-foot mirror in the lobby, as much to make sure my tie is straight as to see if someone is following me in. I really feel, in no particular order: nervous, clueless and stupid. The latter is because I'm here in the first place.

Let's look at this objectively. The good news is that I'm about to spend the evening with an elegant six-foot-tall blond, great legs, wearing the basic black evening dress, and a single strand of pearls, unless she went home and changed. The bad news is that I might get hurt or even worse...killed. The good news is there's a chance that Billy might not even show up. The bad news is that he might. I've run out of good news. And my date is a cop. Hey, it's strictly business. Once again, the lamb to slaughter imagery seems most appropriate. Been there, done that and I still can take nourishment on my own. Bring it on Billy, my lad.

The bar is filled with a combination of registered guests and business folks finishing the day with a cold martini...maybe two and some hot spicy peanuts. A Four Seasons signature dish and in my opinion, one of the best bar munchies ever concocted. Although the recipe is guarded as closely as the crown jewels, suffice it to say that the peanuts are put on a baking sheet, misted with olive oil, baked at 350 for about ten minutes at which time some secret Cajun type spice mixed with salt is sprinkled over the roasted peanuts. Two more minutes in the oven and...perfection. Not only perfect, but the nuts make you so thirsty that you just have to have another drink. Bingo! The people who run the Four Seasons are no dummies.

The routine is fairly straightforward. I order a watered down Grey Goose martini, then a second, then find Detective Browne and pick her up, then make idle conversation for a couple of hours and then we go to a room. All this assumes that Billy doesn't want to join us for a conversation at some point before then.

I saunter up to the bar, mount a stool and signal the bartender. I wonder where Liz is. Instinctively I rub my left ankle with my right foot. It's still there, although I'm not sure how quickly I could get it out of my holster. And the bar is packed. A lot of people are potentially in harm's way and they don't know it.

"May I help you?" The bartender asks. I look up with a start. I didn't even see him coming toward me. I am out of practice for this sort of thing.

"Thank you. I'll have a Grey Goose Martini."

"Shaken or stirred?"

This is not a James Bond guessing game, I hope. Does my answer have anything to do with the plan? No one told me what to say. "Stirred, thank you."

"Olives or onions?"

I'm getting pissed. Now, that's not fair. He's being professional and I should appreciate that he's trying to please a customer. Wait! I'm not a regular customer. He's going to be serving me water. What's the big deal, unless he's not the right bartender.

I hate this. "Two olives, please."

"Very good, sir. I will prepare your martini. Would you care for some peanuts?"

"Yes, thanks." I'm just not a cloak and dagger type cop. Breaking up fights, arresting bad guys, that's what I'm good at. What am I saying, I'm not a cop anymore.

I'll know after the first couple of sips if the Captain's plan is working. Since my drink of choice is beer — domestic from a glass bottle, not a can and never in one of those tall glasses, the taste of vodka will be more pronounced than it might have been a year ago, when I was drinking a bit too much...of everything. Divorce will do that.

People watching is a great pastime, especially in a bar. There is probably enough material for two years worth of sitcoms just in the Four Seasons alone. Where the hell is Liz?

"Sir, your drink. Please give it a taste. If it's too dry, I can add another drop of vermouth." The bartender is either giving me some kind of secret code or he's really good at his job or both.

I raise the chilled glass to my lips. It's water with two olives. "It's perfect."

"Very good. If you want another, just raise your glass and I'll personally make you a refill."

I nod. He scurries away to help another customer. The cacophony of sounds increases in volume as yet another round of drinks is being consumed by the gathered masses.

The tables next to the window overlooking the Public Garden are the first to fill up and are now beginning to turn over as the original occupants move on to their next event.

A couple of men wearing three-piece suits, monogrammed shirts, power ties and carrying leather briefcases, slowly and a bit unsteadily rise to their feet. It's perfect — conveniently nestled in a corner.

Where is the lovely Detective Liz Browne?

You know the expression, no sooner said than done? Within a blink of the eye, Liz slides into one of the seats just vacated by the suits. I hope somebody else doesn't try to pick her up before I do. She's good...really good. Detective Browne places two large shopping bags from a very posh Newbury Street emporium on the chair opposite her, making it impossible for anyone to sashay up and make himself cozy without her consent. I wonder if she actually went shopping while I was freshening up at my apartment? Either she's got a lavish expense account or a sugar daddy. That's ridiculous. She's a successful law enforcement officer who is probably well paid and she can afford her own purchases.

I try not to stare. The truth of the matter is that she is really stunning. Not just pretty, but possessed with a certain presence. Heads turn when she enters a room. I better order my second drink. I look down and notice that my glass is still full. Sipping water doesn't have much appeal. Maybe after a few handfuls of peanuts, I can use the fake martini to quench my thirst.

A mirror runs the entire length of the bar. As

inconspicuously as possible, I scan the room. Other than actually seeing Billy looking at me, what do I expect to see? Power brokers, men cheating on their wives, wives cheating on their husbands, singles looking for something they'll never find in a bar. I am entirely too cynical for my own good. What am I doing in the bar? I'm exposing myself to danger. Get a grip, Callahan. Fantasizing about Liz Browne. See what I mean? No good can come of this.

"May I have another?" I say to the ever-bustling bartender.

"The same as before, sir?" He is good.

"Yes. It was perfect." He nods in response.

How should I do this? Get up and walk directly to her table? Walk around the room and end up at her table? Then what? I am out of practice. What the hell. The Captain's plan has more holes than Swiss cheese. Be direct before some other guy on the prowl tries to hustle the fair Detective Browne. That would really screw things up, getting into a fight with some jerk who is trying to move in on Liz.

"Would like me to run you a tab?" The bartender asks, placing my drink on a fresh napkin.

"Sure. That'll be fine. I'll probably move over to that table with the pretty blonde."

"Well, good luck, sir. I'll tell the waitress to bring you some fresh peanuts." I'm not sure about the protocol regarding tipping the help, especially if they're undercover officers. I decide that not only is leaving a ten-dollar bill appropriate since the service is great, but it looks more authentic. Since I am without a doubt, one of the biggest klutzes around, I decide to take a big sip of my make believe martini...whatever, so that I don't spill it unceremoniously on my shirt while I navigate around the crowd of patrons, which has grown appreciably in the past half hour.

CHAPTER FOURTEEN

"May I?" I gesture at the chair at Liz's table upon which two of the largest shopping bags in the world are resting. What could she possibly have bought? She only had an hour. I remember my ex didn't need more than fifteen minutes to max out not one, but two, credit cards. She was of the school of thought that as long as you had blank checks in your pocketbook, you had money. And balancing her checkbook was not as important as balancing the ratio of gin to dry vermouth in her well-chilled martini glass. Oh well.

"Why not? I'm all alone and the company is welcome," she replies just loud enough for everyone at the bar to hear. I look around, as much to catch a glance of Billy as to gauge the reaction of the assembled masses. No one seems to care.

"Just sit down, sir," she whispers.

"Sir? What's with sir?" I pull the chair back, lift the bags and place them behind Liz. She used her time well. The shopping bags are clearly not props. I note that there are several items all wrapped up in tissue paper. I ease myself into my chair and carefully put my martini glass in the center of the table to reduce the likelihood that I'll knock it over.

If the Captain's plan included the location of the table, his stock has risen in my opinion. The table faces the street so that we can see the foot traffic pass by without being seen because the windows are coated so that they are dark from outside-in, but clear from inside-out. Also there is a large gilded mirror conveniently hanging behind my companion, so I can see the entire room in reverse, while she can see it forward. Actually I am reminded of a story that is told about Fred Astaire and Ginger Rogers. While lauding Astaire's talents, a woman reporter said lest you forget, Ginger is doing it backwards and in high heels.

"Lieutenant...Chris," her voice is lower and coarser than I recalled. Maybe it was the walk in the cold from the Captain's house. I never saw what she was wearing for a coat and her dress hardly constitutes protection from the cold. It hardly constitutes protection from the eye either. She probably checked her coat when she got here. At least her purse is nearby and Commander Marshall made a point of telling me that Detective Browne is a crack shot. Great, I feel better already.

"I'm just another bored suburban housewife who is out on the town, spending her roving-eyed husband's money on Newbury Street, coming in out of the cold to check out the action at the Four Seasons' bar."

Liz is already in character.

"When was the last time you saw Billy O'Brien," she asks professionally and quietly.

"At his trial. A little less than a year ago." I respond.

"According to prison officials, since then, he has grown a beard. Unfortunately, there aren't any recent photos."

"That takes away a bit of our advantage," I say, trying to hide my disappointment. "Did anyone say anything about

Billy's hair?"

"Nothing, so I assume that to mean that it's the same. Why?"

"Billy's hair was so red that some of the older kids in the neighborhood used to call him carrot top, but not for long. He would usually ambush them on the way home from school, one at a time, and beat the shit out of them."

"Nice friend," Detective Browne replies. "Real nice friend."

Suddenly, Liz begins to laugh.

"You're really funny." She pats my hand.

This time a few heads turn, including mine, until it occurs to dumb old me, that this is part of the act. So, I do the natural thing, I take her hand and raise it to my lips and give it an ever so light kiss. I note a little bit of color rising on the face of the lovely detective. Maybe I haven't completely lost my touch.

"I've got a quick question for you," I begin in a normal tone of voice. "Do we have backup in place?" I conclude in a whisper.

"How sweet of you to ask." She places her hand on mine once again. "There are about six undercover units in this room alone, including the bartender. A lot of people are taking this very seriously and everything that could have been done in the time available, has been done. They've been instructed to take no action unless our lives are in danger."

"And?"

"In that event, their orders are to shoot to kill." Liz's tone is all business.

"Very reassuring." As long as they shoot at someone other than me...or Liz.

Trying to use the old Callahan charm seems a total

waste of time. Think about it, how much room is there for small talk when police officers who put themselves on the line are collectively referred to as units or assets. It's like saying casualties rather than hurt or dead people. It's so indifferent. It makes everything sound less real.

I resist the temptation to look around the room. I just hope that Billy doesn't get spooked. There is a fine line between nervous and anxious. I do the logical thing, I take a sip of my virgin martini. Yuck. I resist spitting it out. It's now a tepid virgin martini. I instinctively reach for the peanuts.

"Hey big boy, buy a lady another drink?" Liz slightly slurs her words, successfully breaking the tension.

"Absolutely," I respond, lifting my glass to hers. Our little show is getting some attention because a young woman wearing a black skirt, white blouse and black bow tie scurries over to our table and says, "May I take your order?"

I nod to Liz. I so enjoy her personification of the Stepford Wife. I want to see not only what she orders, but how.

With a wink, addressed at me and not the waitress — I hope, Liz raises her glass and wiggles it just enough so that a little red liquid spills on the white table cloth.

"Oops." A thin smile spreads across her lips — then it's gone. "I know why everyone says you serve the best Bloody Marys in town. I'd like another. Join me...handsome?"

"Handsome? I think that's a bit over the top." I mumble under my breath.

"Not really." She smiles again.

It's my turn to blush. Addressing the waitress, I say, "Another one of these, please."

"Very good madam, sir. I've been told to place it on

your tab, sir." I hope the waitress is giving me a little sign that she's in on this...whatever this is.

"Fine, and may we have some more peanuts?" I look at the empty bowl. I guess I'm hungrier than I thought.

"Why don't we get something real to eat?" Liz whispers.

"Good call," I respond. "I'm sure the Captain's plan includes a wonderful meal."

"A girl's got to keep up her strength and besides, I didn't get wined and dined at Locke-Ober."

"Waitress, may we have a couple of menus?" I ignore Liz's slight jab about lunch.

"I'll put in your drink orders and return with menus. Do you want to see the wine list or would you prefer to stay with your cocktails?" There is no doubt that the waitress is part of our team, which consists of...whoever. Always more questions than answers.

"This could be fun if we weren't waiting for a psychopath to surprise us." Liz is talking from behind a small makeup mirror she removed from her purse.

"We'll have to do it again. Soon,I hope," sounding as confident as circumstances permit.

"It's my turn, can I ask you a question?" Liz leans toward me. "Why did you leave the force? By all accounts you were a great cop and a real hero."

"It's a long story, but the short version is that people were always shooting at me and while it is part of the job, the frequency was increasing despite my efforts to stay in one piece. After being hit, albeit in the ass, I thought the odds had suddenly changed and not in my favor. Also, I was hoping to have a family and I didn't want to leave a widow, and kids without a father." My retort sounded logical without being too standoffish.

"But your wife left you."

"And went to live with my former partner. That hurt, but doesn't change the underlying premise that survival has a large dose of luck mixed in and when you've used up your share of luck — change jobs." It seems easy to talk about...now.

The waitress reappears with menus. "We have several specials tonight. May I tell you about them?" Food is sounding very good just now. We both nod.

CHAPTER FIFTEEN

The food at the Bristol, the Four Seasons' restaurant, is about as good as it gets in Boston, although lunching at Locke-Ober is still a pretty special treat. I'm either a glutton or a gourmand. Either way, I enjoy good food, good ambiance, good service and good company, preferably without the lingering thought that serious danger is lurking around the corner.

"Sir?" Our waitress snaps me out of this momentary trance.

"Sorry." It's the best I can come up with on such short notice.

"Tonight Chef Thomas (pronounced "toe-mas") has outdone himself." I wonder if she starts out describing the food the same way every night or is she playacting like the rest of us? Maybe this is her first waitperson job and she's trying to wing it. That assumes she's a cop, too.

"In addition to the items that appear on our menu, we are featuring as a starter, Ahi Tuna Poke with rainbow radish, toasted sesame seeds, wasabi and wonton crisps." She pauses as I try to assimilate the ingredients.

The menu at Locke-Ober is far less challenging. The food is simple, elegant but understated. I know what something will taste like before I order, not after I get it.

"For a main course, we have Pappardelle."

I hope she doesn't confuse my plebian palate with boorishness.

"A sautéed Vermont chicken served with oven cured tomatoes, capers, shallots, oregano and Pecorino Romano," she finishes.

"May we have a few minutes to consider the specials, as well as the regular menu offerings?" Liz is actually making a statement rather than asking a question.

"Of course…take your time…the kitchen doesn't close until ten." The waitress flashes a brief smile.

I really wish I could get a look at the wine list. It seems a shame to dine without wine. Hey, that rhymes. Better not give up my day job, which is…I'm not entirely sure anymore.

"There are a lot of wonderful-sounding dishes on the menu and I know what most of them are." I think that Liz is getting into the food mood.

I struggle to open the menu, which seems unnecessarily large. Maybe it's to impress patrons. I think that if they want big menus, the least they could do is increase the size of the print so that those of us with aging eyes don't have to squint to read. I may have to give in and visit my local Wal-Mart and pick up a pair of cheaters — reading glasses.

Liz is right. There are some offerings on the menu that might fill the emptiness I feel in the pit of my stomach.

"Have you decided?" My dining companion is either very courteous or very hungry. Actually, she probably didn't get any lunch. What a set-up. The Captain knows me too well. The best way to get to Chris Callahan is through his stomach.

"Actually, it's between two things. What are you going to order?" I ask.

"Beet salad and veal tenderloin with..." she looks back down at the menu. "...wheat berry tabouleh, pine nuts, dates, rapini, roasted tomatoes and lemon-clove jus." She starts to laugh.

"I think I know what you're going to be eating, but I'm not entirely sure. I've decided. Clam chowdah and filet of beef — medium."

"Chris, I think you have another choice to make." Once again Liz raises the menu to read. She reminds of my third grade teacher, Sister Judith, taking roll each morning. "This is very important, so pay attention." I can tell that she is trying to prevent herself from bursting out in laughter. "You may select either creamy horseradish Yukon potatoes or truffle Parmesan fries." She lowers the menu. "Which shall it be?"

"You mean I've gotta choose between mashed potatoes and French fries? That's a no brainer. In an Irish household on Sundays, Tuesdays and Thursdays you get boiled potatoes and on Mondays, Wednesdays and Saturdays you eat mashed potatoes, which were the left-over boiled potatoes from the night before. French fries were a treat, saved for Fridays — fish and chips — no ketchup, only vinegar. Gross."

By this time, Liz is laughing so hard that she begins to turn red. "You are the funniest person I've ever met."

"I think you must then know some of the dullest people on the planet." I reply.

"I do. I really do."

We are both laughing so hard that if anyone is looking, I'm sure they'll have no trouble finding us. We're the ones making all the noise.

At least we got the waitress' attention. "Have you made your selections?"

"Yes, thank you. My dear, please order." I try to sound almost over the top.

Liz picks up her menu and repeats her selections. I do the same. The waitress smiles and leaves. I look down and see a piece of paper. I didn't remember the waitress dropping anything, although I admit I was spending more time stifling a laugh than concentrating on our waitperson. I slowly unfold the plain white sheet of paper.

"Shit!"

Liz looks up. "What?"

"Read this." I hand her the paper.

"Where did it come from?"

"I just noticed it after we ordered." The inflection of my voice reflects the concern I feel.

"Chris, it's no big deal. All the note says is "ENJOY". Maybe it's from the management. You know, like after you order. Kind of like a thanks for ordering note."

"Liz, you don't believe that for a minute, do you? It's written with a marking pen. I'm more concerned with how it got here."

"Excuse me." Liz gets up. "I've got to go to the ladies' room." I start to stand. "Be right back." She blows me a kiss.

There are probably a lot of envious guys in the bar about now. I can't tell if Liz is role-playing or enjoying my company.

I guess until we hook up with Billy or give up, I really won't know. The note has unnerved me. I look into the room...backwards. No red hair and a beard. Has he gained any weight? That can change a person's appearance, too. I count about eight men in their late thirties with dark hair and a beard, but none has Billy's pale blue eyes. That can't change, unless he's wearing color contacts. I'm not making a lot of progress. I see Liz returning. Once again I begin to stand, but she places a hand on my shoulder.

"Miss me?"

Playacting or the real thing?

"Unimaginably," I reply. I raise my fake martini in toast. "Here's looking at you babe." Liz touches the rim of her equally fake Bloody Mary to my glass.

"If you want me, just whistle. You do know how to whistle...don't you?" She makes a far better Lauren Bacall than I do a Humphrey Bogart. Before Liz finishes the punch line, we both break out in laughter. It helps relieve the tension.

"The note came from inside your menu. It was placed there by someone dressed to look like a busboy immediately before our waitress brought them over to the table." I wonder if Liz learned all this in the ladies' room. I raise one eyebrow. "The entire room is under video surveillance. I asked one of our contacts on the way into the john and had the answer on the way out."

I've never heard a woman calling the ladies' room — a john. She's my kind of girl. I'm getting ahead of myself. I look into the mirror to see if I can see any busboys. Wait!

"What did the busboy look like? If it's caught on video, maybe we can get a print."

"Not much help there. Busboy is Hispanic, 5' 4" and about twenty."

That eliminates Billy. A 6-foot-tall Irishman couldn't pass.

Liz's words are not encouraging. "I've asked our contact to follow up and see if she can find out who told the busboy to put the note in the menu, although he'll probably feign memory loss, assuming he's a real employee of the restaurant."

"At least we know Billy is out there." I don't sound as sure of myself as I should.

"Let's hope that it is Billy." Liz's retort surprises me. I wonder if she knows something I don't. Probably. No real surprise. I think I'll let it slide. Our food arrives...just in time.

CHAPTER SIXTEEN

There's something about a steaming bowl of real New England clam chowder. To me and probably to anyone who is a real Bostonian, chowder is the ultimate comfort food. Until I was about twenty, I never knew that there were actually two soups, each claiming the title clam chowder. The good old-fashioned, made-from-cream white chowder — and a red imitator, made from tomatoes and, not surprisingly, called Manhattan clam chowder. I have long suspected that George Steinbrenner invented Manhattan clam chowder to compete with our chowder. Kind of like the Yankees and the Red Sox.

I have never been a beet fan, although my mom served them often enough when we were growing up. I put them in the same category as spinach — good for you — but both taste terrible. I think that the way my mom prepared vegetables has a lot to do with it. Al dente was the name of the local barber, not the way vegetables were prepared. Bad joke, but at least I still have my sense of humor to go along with my sense of dread.

"How's your chowder?" Liz's question snaps me out of my trip down memory lane. Thinking about Billy O'Brien has made me remember a lot of things I haven't thought about in years.

"It's great. Want a taste?"

"Please." I look around for another spoon, decide that a teaspoon doesn't do the chowder justice and dip my soup spoon deep into the bowl, making sure I get a clam. Liz moves her face toward the oncoming spoon and deftly sips its contents — clam and all.

"Fabulous. Want to try a bite of my salad? The sweetness of the beets is offset by the tanginess of the vinaigrette."

"No thanks, I'm not a beet guy." I smile.

"Your mom probably overcooked them. Mine did. But properly prepared, beets are really tasty and good for you." Liz is slowly, maybe not so slowly, finding her way into my heart...assuming I still have one. "A little bite?"

"Okay, you've twisted my arm." I lean over the table toward the awaiting fork. I remove the contents without gagging and without clicking my teeth on the tines of the fork — a major no-no in our house. I am thinking about my childhood a lot today. "Not bad," I add. Actually, it wasn't bad.

Our repartee is interrupted by another waitperson. "Sir, the wine list." He places a leather covered book in front of me and quickly retires before I can ask him a couple of questions, like we already told our waitress that we weren't having wine, but staying with our fake drinks. Maybe he's the sommelier and nobody told him we had passed on the wine list. He's just doing his job. I'm a little paranoid. I might as well take a look and see what we're missing. A quick glance at Liz and I get the feeling that she is equally surprised.

"Chris, what's going on?"

"I'm not sure, but there's no harm in looking at the list.

It may be no more than an overly efficient waiter."

Wrong. My eyes immediately focus on a single white piece of paper upon which is written in black marker Try the Malbec. I pick it up by a corner and pass it to Liz.

"Not altogether unexpected." Her voice was cold and flat.

"Explain...please." I look at her.

"If Billy wants to get in touch with you, he's not going to pull up a chair and sit down. You know, order a beer. He's sending little messages to let you know he's around. He wants to see what you're going to do, how you react."

I lift my hand to summon our waitperson. Our regular waitress, who seems to be in the know, and another waiter with a silver salver worn on a silver chain arrive at the same time.

Voilà, the real sommelier. "I would like to order some wine." I close the list. Liz places her napkin over the note.

Our waitress ever so slightly raises one of her eyebrows, while the sommelier politely says, "Have you decided or can I help you with some suggestions?"

"I think we'd like a Malbec." I look up at Liz, who nods.

"We have a very nice 2004 Palumba from Argentina."

"Perfect." I love ordering without considering the price.

Both waitpersons leave.

"Chris, I don't think we have to be concerned. If Billy is out there and I have every reason to believe that he is, he won't actually make physical contact in a way that will draw attention to himself. What most concerns me, is whether someone is following Billy, or conversely, whether someone is following us to get at Billy. I know it's a remote possibility, but I'm not as positive as everyone else that there's not a second scenario being acted out at the same time. I'm not sure by whom."

"What are you saying?"

"Okay. Let's say that Billy is playing on both sides of the street. The Feds assume his true loyalty is to them, but up until a couple of hours ago, I'd wager that you were completely convinced that Billy's loyalties lay with the bad guys." I'm not entirely sure where Liz is going, but I don't like the sound of it.

"I agree that to the outside world, Billy looks like a hood." That's the best I can come up with.

"You weren't the rest of the world. You were a long time friend and a cop. A very good cop and he looked like a hood to you, too."

"True. That's why the murders didn't surprise me. Maybe that's why I didn't look past Billy." I am beginning to doubt my own judgment. Not a good sign.

At the Four Seasons, food and wine presentation is as important as preparation. In addition to our regular server, each table is attended by a wine steward. Rounding off the team is an assistant server, whose only role seems to be to ensure that each patron has the proper number of knives, forks and spoons.

Our sommelier approaches with sweeping gestures, heretofore saved for movies starring Grace Kelly. He presents a bottle for my approval. Three watered-down martinis is all I can handle. Odds are Captain Hancock is enjoying a glass of something stronger. Liz seems to read my mind. She points at her still-empty wine glass and smiles. Our server extracts the cork, which he closely examines, regardless of the fact that it's not real, it's plastic. At least it's not a screw top, although I am told that many high-end vineyards are beginning to bottle with reusable caps. This is a new twist on turning water into wine.

Our sommelier pours a perfectly measured portion of wine into his silver salver, swirls the red liquid, smells the bouquet, appreciates the legs and adjudicates it fit to drink. He pours a measured portion into my glass for approval. Although I'm a guy from Southie where long neck Buds are considered grand cru, I can act the part,,,sometimes. As I recall, Malbec is a rather moderately priced high altitude varietal, usually from South America, costing less than $20 a bottle, in a package store. Rather elaborate for cheap wine, but very impressive and Liz is smiling. I swirl, sniff and sip.

"Very nice. Thanks," I say nodding to the anxiously awaiting server, who pours a larger measure into Liz's glass and then tops up mine. The partially empty bottle is then swaddled in a linen napkin and placed at the edge of the table…far enough away to discourage self-service. The head server removes our now empty salad plates and soup bowls. The trio retreats.

"To you." I raise my glass.

"To us," Liz responds. We both take a sip — a very small sip. It seems that we both have silently and simultaneously acknowledged the gravity of our situation. We must keep our wits about us, but it is easy to forget when I look across at Liz.

"Thank you for ordering the wine," Liz comments.

"I didn't, Billy did."

We clink glasses ever so lightly and bring the glasses to our respective lips…and sip.

CHAPTER SEVENTEEN

Suddenly I feel a vibration. An instant before I reach for my ankle holster, I realize that it's my cell phone.

"Excuse me," I say to Liz and flip open the cover. It's not an iPhone, but it always works. "Callahan."

Liz leans forward.

"When?" I pause. "Thanks. I'll keep you posted. Love to the kids." I close the cell phone with a snap and return it to my pocket.

"Are you going to share the conversation with me?" Liz's voice brings me back into focus.

"That was my sister, Maureen. She still lives in the old neighborhood. Billy was seen coming out of church. Go figure."

"When?"

"Around 8:30 this morning, after Mass."

"And then?"

"Nothing. Poof. Maureen asked around and no one has seen him since then. Damn!"

"Chris," Liz tries to sound cheerful. "That's good news. At least we know that he's around and that the notes we are getting are probably from Billy."

Why doesn't this news make me feel warm and fuzzy?

"Billy going to church. It doesn't fit." I'm not sure I know where I'm going with this.

"That's because your Billy is the punk kid turned hood and not what may be the other Billy." Liz makes sense but I'm still not reassured.

In the back of my subconscious, I hear a voice.

"Excuse me." I look up and see our waitperson and her assistant holding our entrees.

"Sorry, we were absorbing the ambiance of our surroundings." Sounds convincing and it's better than admitting you are an airhead.

With practiced efficiency, Liz's veal and my filet of beef are placed before us. I wonder if the BPD has special officer training in being a waitperson or a bartender? It is unbelievable that food can be such an art form. Not only is the presentation worthy of inclusion in the Louvre, but the taste is beyond description. Thanks Captain. I only hope this isn't my last meal...with Liz or my last meal...period.

Liz and I chat about everything and nothing. It is obvious we are making conversation to take our minds off the task at hand. Which is...what? I think that despite all the assurances we extracted from our colleagues, our role is limited. We are Judas goats. "Chris." Liz's voice once again brings me back to the here and now. "Nothing is going to happen at dinner. Please eat before it gets cold."

I sheepishly look down at my filet and fries. She's right. Eat, drink and be merry for tomorrow we may die. What a lousy thought. I raise my still full glass of wine. "To tomorrow."

"And many other tomorrows," Liz adds. I feel better already.

We clink our glasses again and each take a healthy belt of wine.

Not bad. I'll have to remember to order Malbec again... with Liz.

My dinner beckons.

After a couple minutes of culinary exotica, I ask, "Want a bite?"

"Only if you have a bite of mine," Liz retorts. I think I love her. With just a few well-chosen words, she takes a situation from awkward to comfortable, unless she's really coming on to me. Callahan, wake up. The prize is survival and if you accomplish that, then you can think about getting on with State Police Detective Browne, but not before.

I cut a piece of meat, stab it elegantly (tines down) and present it for tasting.

"Wow. That is good. Here, try this." Liz duplicates my routine.

It's funny, I'm a basic steak and potatoes guy, but I never got into veal. Maybe because when we were kids, veal was always expensive or maybe it was the basically inhumane process of fattening the calves for slaughter. That's not fair to dairy farmers. What else can you do with male cows or is it cattle?

I lean over and deftly remove the piece of meat. It doesn't taste like beef at all. It's good. Very good, but different. I might learn to acquire a taste for veal.

"Thanks." I smile. "Wow, beets and veal in one meal."

"Would you like some more wine?" The sommelier had approached so quietly that I visibly jump, again. I've got to remain vigilant and focused.

"Just a touch." Liz's glass has already been refilled, which means I missed the entire exchange between the wine steward and Liz. Tuning in and out like an old AM car radio, will certainly qualify me for admission to the local funny farm or make me a candidate for the morgue. Neither is very appealing, thank you very much.

CHAPTER EIGHTEEN

"I can't believe I'm that stupid!"

"What are you talking about?" Liz's reply immediately follows my outburst.

"I forgot to ask my sister what Billy looks like." I can feel the blood rushing to my head.

"Call her back. His appearance can't have changed that much if he was recognized coming out of church."

"You're right. I'm grasping at straws."

"Duh! We're both scared shitless. Well at least I am." Liz has a way of putting things in context.

"I'm going to call Maureen anyway," I reply.

"Take a deep breath before you dial. She doesn't know what we are up to, so there is no point in creating panic."

"You are so damn reasonable."

"A lady's role is to calm down her man." Her smile lights up the entire room…at least my portion of it.

I open my cell phone and speed dial Maureen's number. One ring…two rings…three rings. Shit! What's her cell number? "Maureen, glad I caught you. I forgot to ask, did anyone mention what Billy looks like? You know, like does he have a beard or long hair or has he gained or lost weight?" Liz leans close to me. Her perfume smells divine, but if I let her distract me, divinity will be the only thing we'll have.

"That's a good idea. How long will it take?" I am less than happy with Maureen's response, but I know she's right. "Okay, call just as soon as you know…whenever. Thanks."

Liz leans back in her chair and raises one eyebrow just a smidge. You know the gesture. Tell me everything…now.

"She'll make some calls and see what she can find out. It's getting late, especially for morning Mass attendees, whose average age is north of seventy. Maureen never saw Billy. The good news, if there is any, is that people sense there's enough friction between the two of us that they felt that it was important to get a message to me that he's back."

"Did your sister say whether anyone talked to him?"

"No! Damn it, I forgot to ask."

"Chris, don't be so hard on yourself." Liz says. "Let's finish dinner and keep with the plan. So far, so good."

"You mean so far Billy hasn't whacked us."

"We don't know what he wants, so don't be all negative. It serves no purpose. We have every reason to assume that the notes have come from Billy. They have not been threatening."

"I disagree. I think that the notes have been a very subtle form of intimidation. Like…I know where you are but you don't know where I am. Ha! Ha!"

"Chris. Shut up and eat your food." Liz winks

"Yes 'em." I take a bite of filet, then a couple of French fries. Yuck, they're cold. Before I say a word, our server is at the table.

"Sir? Would you like some warm potatoes? They do seem to get cold on one's plate in the wink of an eye."

I wonder if she's referring to Liz's wink or just the basic, generic wink?

"Yes, please. I am very partial to hot fries."

"Very good, sir." She hustles off.

"My compliments to your Captain," Liz says. "This is the classiest stakeout I've ever been on."

"Why detective, we were told that the State Police dine like this on every stakeout." My smile doesn't radiate as brightly as hers, but it is just as sincere.

"Touché." She lifts her glass.

"Only a sip. Remember, we are on duty."

"Oh my...perish the thought."

"Yours or mine?"

Liz's laughter draws a lot of attention. Tears are streaking down her cheek. "If Billy O'Brien is anywhere within a two block radius, he'll know we're here," she says gasping for air.

"This is a lot more fun than painting a target on our backs and walking through the Public Garden." I'm not very good at comebacks, if it isn't already obvious. But I am having fun and I've got a full plate of hot French fries, which I don't have to share. A server slides a heaping pile of steaming potatoes next to me.

"Enjoy."

I look down at the plate, then at the retreating back of the person who placed them on the table. Then I looked down again. I'm really getting pissed off at Billy O'Brien. Stop leaving me dumb notes. I was so preoccupied with charming Ms. Browne that I hadn't noticed that the server was neither our regular waitperson, who is somehow on our team, nor her assistant, who was at least neutral, but yet another message carrier. Liz glances over and realizes that there is something amiss.

"Chris, what is it?"

"Another personalized note."

"Personalized?"

"Have a look." I push the note toward Liz with the eraser end of a pencil I carry in my sport coat pocket.

"He really knows you, doesn't he?"

"Pretty obvious we shared a lot of our childhood."

"He's very clever."

"Deadly clever."

"Let's hope not. TGIF — don't forget the malt vinegar doesn't sound threatening. It's actually charming." Liz only knows a paper Billy O'Brien, not the real Billy O'Brien, but then again, I'm not sure I know the real Billy O'Brien either. What I do know is that when we were kids he'd come over for fish and chips every Friday night, cooked only the way my mom could. If his purpose is to let me know he's watching, he has succeeded. This note could only be from Billy.

"Excuse me," I literally grab a passing server. "May I have some ketchup for my fries?" The waitperson nods. "Thanks," I remark to her back as she retreats to wherever condiments are kept.

Across the table, Liz is cutting a piece of veal. "Bon appetit."

I raise my fork in a mock salute. "Life is too short to eat cold French fries." I spear a mouthful. They are really good.

"And to drink cheap wine." Liz tilts her glass ever so slightly toward me.

CHAPTER NINETEEN

The meal is really over-the-top good. Food, wine and the pleasure of a lovely lady's company can make one feel complacent. Way too complacent for the danger lurking out there...somewhere. At least there have been no more notes and the phone hasn't rung.

I think I'd feel better if I heard from my sister. It might give me some idea of what...who to look for. Liz senses my apprehension. Just the simple gesture of wiping her mouth is deliberate. Not sexy deliberate, but classy deliberate.

Both of our plates are spotlessly clean. I guess we were either hungry or nervous or both. I've just made an executive decision. Based on the well-documented fact that people eat more when they are under stress, for which this situation clearly qualifies, hereafter I am only going to eat at expensive restaurants with beautiful women. I'm not sure how my accountant is going to handle the expense. Should it be itemized as meals and entertainment or medical — like therapy? In any event, it will be deductible.

I'm rudely brought back to the here and now by a vibrating sensation. Damn, it's only my cell phone.

"Callahan." I think that my voice sounds a bit edgy. "Oh, hi. Thanks for getting back to me. Sorry, I didn't mean to sound testy. I forgot to look at the caller ID." I pause to listen.

"That's interesting. Who'd have thought? You're great to have been so thorough. Love you too." I flip the phone closed and look up.

Liz's eyebrow is raised into the what's going on position.

"It was Maureen. She talked to four of the early Mass regulars. They all have senior memory moments. No surprise, but they all remember seeing Billy and commenting that he looks exactly the same as when he stole the Cadillac. You got to love them. They can't remember who is president, but they remember every detail of Billy's joy ride."

"At least we know what he looks like," Liz replies.

"I hope so."

"You're not sure?"

"I'm not ruling out a disguise. Remember, he's been watching us rather up close and personal without being too conspicuous. I haven't seen anybody who even looks remotely like Billy. Red hair should be easy to spot."

"Would you like to view our dessert offerings?" Although the service is fabulous at The Four Seasons, under the circumstances I am just a bit sensitive to people sneaking up on me.

"Chris?" Liz's voice faintly resonates.

"Sorry. I zoned out...again."

"Quite understandable. However, I think we should scope out the sweets."

"I haven't heard someone call desserts sweets since my grandmother. And she didn't look a thing like you."

I guess the Billy thing has got me reminiscing about a world I left a long time ago. There were reasons then and they still seem valid now, albeit less intense. Life marches on to the beat of a distant drum. Way too deep for a time like this.

"Do you have a dessert menu?" I ask the waitperson.

"No sir, we have a trolley." She beckons her assistant across the room.

I lift my glass and tip it ever so slightly toward Liz.

"To the Captain...to our mission...and to Billy, wherever he may be." I hope I don't sound like the best man at a cheesy wedding.

"To us," she replies.

I will never forgive myself if I get killed tonight. How selfish. Liz is at risk as much as I am. This might be as good of a time as any to say one of those 'God, if you get me out of this mess I'll never do anything wrong again or I'll go to church every Sunday or...'

"Chris, there's no way I can eat an entire piece of... anything. Will you share?" There is nothing coy about Liz's voice. It is sincere, very trusting.

Eight plates are magnificently presented on the dessert cart. Each looks better than the other. Quick thinking Callahan says, "Everything looks great. You decide."

Detective Browne furrows her brow in deep concentration, points and says, "Key lime pie. My favorite. Okay?"

"Perfect choice," I respond. And it is. I love key lime pie, although I would prefer to be eating it in Key West — over a thousand miles from here and from Billy.

CHAPTER TWENTY

I've just had an epiphany. Not food-inspired, although I wish I had ordered my own portion of key lime pie, but much greater and far-reaching. It has suddenly dawned on me that I really hate sitting around, waiting for someone else to do something, especially when I am basically a sitting duck if anyone decides to do something bad. I do not like being used as a pawn in someone else's game. In fact, I'm getting pissed off. Not at Liz, whose company I am enjoying, but that I'm up to my ass in a problem that isn't my problem. I didn't cause it, unless arresting a criminal or purported criminal in the line of duty, makes it my problem, which is absolute crap. I did my job. Someone else or maybe a lot of someone elses screwed up and I'm supposed to fix it and in the process, more likely than not, get myself and the lovely Detective Browne seriously, maybe permanently, injured.

I don't mind a good old-fashioned bar fight and I've shot my share of bad guys, but waiting until something happens and not doing anything about it doesn't cut it. Chris Callahan may be a lot of things, but a thick-headed Irishman from Southie who does nothing but leisurely sip fine wines while an escaped convict is writing cute notes isn't what Mother

Callahan had in mind.

"Liz, let's go!" I quickly stand up, look around and walk around to her side of the table.

"Aren't we supposed to wait for awhile until O'Brien has had time to make contact with us." Liz speaks altogether too fast.

"Please just get up." I give her chair a tug.

She tries to resist. Liz is clearly confused by my otherwise unexpected action.

"But…"

"Now!" I don't want to draw more attention to us than is absolutely necessary. Slowly, she pushes the chair back.

"Chris…what's going…"

"Liz, just do as I say, please." She nods.

I grab her shopping bags and glance inside. Other than a lot of tissue paper, only a pair of gray sweats fills one bag, while the other has some personal items. So much for the shopping spree theory.

Seeing the quizzical look on my face, she says, "You didn't expect me to sleep in my dress did you?"

Inasmuch as there is a certain sense of urgency in my movements, I didn't quip that I sleep in the nude. It didn't seem like the appropriate thing to say.

"Just follow me." I grab her elbow, probably a little too hard, and guide her to the coatroom to retrieve her coat.

"Our orders are to stay here tonight." Liz speaks between clenched teeth.

"I don't follow orders. Remember? I'm an insubordinate ex-cop and I am relying on my gut to get us out of here."

"But the plan?"

"Detective, the purpose of the plan was to make contact with Billy. It is obvious that based on the number of notes we got during our dinner charade, Billy has made contact with us."

"Fair enough. That's the plan and it's working."

I hope Liz doesn't misconstrue the detective comment. She needs to think like a cop. We have a job to do and we need to be focused, especially when it's a matter of life and death. And it did get her attention. "Get your coat. We're out of here."

"Chris?"

"Just do what I say. Please." I give her hand a squeeze as much to reassure me as to reassure her.

With great reluctance, I release her hand and head over to the valet-parking clerk, hand him my check and a twenty. "It's the classic Chevy. Shouldn't be hard to find."

I smell Liz before I see or hear her. "Shouldn't we tell someone we're leaving?" she asks. Uncertainty is easy to spot. It's like never showing fear when confronted by a dog. Sounds good, but try it sometime, especially if the dog is two-legged.

"Listen, probably everybody in the city of Boston knows where we are and who we are and I've learned from the school of hard knocks that we need home court advantage."

"I'm not sure I follow." Uncertainty again.

"Just stay close. Do what I say, when I say it and we may just live to see tomorrow. Trust me."

Liz's nod does not exude confidence, but she doesn't resist either.

"Sir?" The valet has been trying to get my attention for I don't know how long. "Your car?" He opens the door for Liz, who unhesitatingly gets in...without comment.

"Thanks." I hand the valet another twenty. Who cares? If we make it through the night, I'll add it to my expense account, if not, no big deal.

I slide in. "Buckle up."

"Yes, sir." Is that a smile I see?

"Shit!"

"What's wrong?"

"I wasn't paying attention. Look!" I point to the corner of the windshield. I guess I thought it was the valet ticket, but it's not. It's another fuckin' note. At least I have the presence of mind to stop the car before I pull out into traffic, get out and carefully lift the piece of paper from under the wiper.

Don't trust anybody...anybody.

Great advice, under the circumstances.

"May I see?" I carefully hand her the latest epistle.

"Ironic, isn't it?" Liz has regained her composure. She is really something special.

"Why, because I just asked you to trust me?"

She nods.

"Do you?"

"Trust you?"

"Yes."

"A lot. Let's go...wherever."

I ease the car onto Boylston Street and bully my way across four lanes so that I can cut between the Garden and the Commons, take a left onto Beacon and right onto the Storrow Drive ramp.

"We're going to my apartment in Cambridge. It's safe and it may give us an advantage.Over whom, I'm not sure."

"I don't understand." Liz is articulating what I'm feeling.

"Too much information about us got out too quickly. There's no way Billy O'Brien could have found out on his own that we were at the Four Seasons."

"An informer?"

"How does an inside informer sound?"

"That validates the argument that Billy may have been working for the Feds and they really want to talk to him."

"May I suggest another possibility?" I take a quick glance toward my passenger. That's all the time one can take while in Boston, trying to avoid cars, guardrails, debris and other obstacles that litter its roads.

"I'm all ears." Liz cups her hand to hear.

I try not to laugh. Thank God she brought a sweat suit. If I don't start concentrating we'll be a traffic statistic rather than a homicide. Great options. "If the note we just got is from Billy, and please note I said if, then he is telling us he's not the source of our danger."

"Maybe he is telling you not to trust me."

"Ms. Browne, you're the one who hopped into my car with nothing but two shopping bags, whose contents I've seen and a small, albeit deadly, handgun in your purse. I think I'm safe."

"You've never seen me in my custom-fitting gray Northeastern University official athletic outerwear. Maybe you'll die of laughter."

"Wow! Now I am worried. Okay, I'll officially take you off my list of suspects."

A blast from a car horn reminds me that I had better pay attention to my driving. I quickly look around and am relieved to note that someone else was the object of the irate honker. I glance up into the rear view mirror to see if anyone is obviously following us. I switch lanes, without using my turn signals, and slow down.

"Chris, what's wrong?" I guess the State police never gave Detective Browne the shake a tail driving course. I probably could have put that another way, but at least I'm talking to myself.

"I'm just checking to see if anyone is following us." That didn't sound quite as bad.

"See anything?"

"Nothing obvious, but if we are dealing with pros, be they good guys or bad guys, then nothing is going to be obvious."

"But going back to your place is not obvious?"

"You've got a point, but it's my house and just wait until you see the joint. We will be reasonably secure and able to defend ourselves. And besides, it's fully equipped with a fireplace, wine cellar, six burner Viking range and fully stocked Sub-Zero refrigerator."

"Are you planning on being under siege?"

"I hope not, but on the bright side, with six burners we can heat up the boiling oil to pour down on the unwashed hoard of attackers and have a cold beer at the same time."

"Can we use it to heat up some water? I would love a cup of tea."

CHAPTER TWENTY-ONE

For the sake of giving anyone who might be following us a chance to show themselves, I decide to add a few extra miles and a lot of extra turns on the trip to my apartment. Not only will the extra time give me a chance to devise a plan — any plan at this point, but it will make tailing us more difficult. Also, the longer and twistier the journey, the more likely a follower will slip up. I don't want to lose the tail, especially if it's Billy. I just want to confirm my instincts. Small talk seems a bit trite, so I slip a Diana Krall CD into my only compromise to modernity in the car. As Long as I Live, featuring a fabulous bass and piano solo, fills the Chevy.

"Nice, very nice." Detective Browne purrs. She is either relaxing or she is very much on edge.

"I've been a fan of her music since way before she became popular. I remember a concert when Diana Krall opened for Tony Bennett. What a night." It suddenly occurs to me that I recall every song from the concert, but I cannot remember who I went with. Weird or scary.

"Knock, knock, Mr. Callahan, are you there?"

"I've decided to drive around a bit to see if someone is actually following us or whether I'm being more paranoid than normal."

Without benefit of turn signal, I turn up the Allston exit, take a left where the Coca Cola plant used to be, and head down toward the Harvard Business School. People in New England, especially in Boston, give directions using places that no longer exist as points of reference. Coupled with poor street signage, it is a wonder that more people don't get lost. Since the road you are on is never identified by a sign, navigation is by cross streets only, which can be a bit confusing and frustrating, which explains the inordinately high incidences of urban road rage.

"See anyone?" Liz is somewhat less relaxed, glancing into the side view mirror.

"Not sure," I reply. My eyes shift from the rear view mirror, to the road, to Liz, to the side view mirror and back to the road. It would be in bad form to crash into a parked car.

I execute right and left turns randomly, while remaining on the Boston side of the Charles River. I want to keep up this routine for about five minutes, making sure that I remain only a couple of miles from my apartment...in case. In case of what? I am going to drive myself crazy. Diana Krall singing The Look of Love under another set of circumstances would be perfect. I steal a quick glance at Liz. Her lips are moving to the words.

"Do you think Billy knows where you live?" Detective Browne may have been temporarily lost in the song, but immediately returns to the real world.

"I'm in the book." I try to sound reassuring.

"Then why are we driving around?"

"To see if Billy is following us and more importantly to see if someone is following Billy if he is following us.

Maybe someone is simply following us hoping we will lead them to Billy."

"Why don't we go to your apartment and see who turns up?"

"I was hoping to get some idea of the number of players in the game first."

"You mean in addition to your Captain, my Commander and the two Feds?"

"Don't forget Billy."

"And whomever you think may be following Billy."

"As I recall, I never said there's someone else following Billy. That suggestion came from my dear friend Pete." I am searching for the boundaries that define this case. There are too many potential people involved. Might as well go home and set up camp.

"Chris, I am worried. Not the I'm afraid of getting hurt kind of worried, but the who are the good guys and who are the bad guys kind of worried."

"If it is of any consolation, I have had the same feeling since I had lunch with Captain Hancock and Commander Marshall and it's not getting any better."

"This is a mess."

I nod as I glance up into the rear view mirror.

"We are not alone and haven't been for awhile," I announce. "There are a pair of unmarked cars that have been following us alternately so that I don't pick them out. There may be a third car as well. I am getting concerned."

"You are not making me feel encouraged." Liz sounds worried. I suspect that most of her police work has been riding a desk, not shotgun in a cruiser.

"It's my problem, not yours." I sound very casual.

"What do you mean by that?" There is an edge in her voice.

"It's not your problem that I don't have enough clean wine glasses to serve all these people if they show up at the same time."

My sense of humor is awarded by a huge laugh. The tension-breaking type of laugh.

"They probably drink beer out of a can anyway."

"Then they will be out of luck. I am a long-neck guy."

"And long legs, I hope." Liz slides one of her legs over the other, showing just the correct amount of thigh. A practiced move.

"And long legs." I turn left onto North Harvard Street and head for the Square — Harvard Square. Only one set of headlights follows. The other turns right.

CHAPTER TWENTY-TWO

Either they have figured out that I've spotted them or they don't care. Each time one set of headlights peels off the rear view mirror, another identical pair appears. Traffic into and out of Harvard Square is heavy, redefining the meaning of bumper to bumper. I can almost make out the features of my current tail. The good news is that I don't recognize him. The bad news is that I don't recognize him, unless it's a her in a serious disguise. The vehicle is a light gray Ford Crown Victoria, the law enforcement car of choice. If my companion was a Lincoln Town Car, I might be more worried. A Lincoln is the car of choice of non-law enforcement personnel. Cadillacs are considered way too showy.

Liz has become very quiet. "Where is your place?" she asks softly.

"Couple of blocks," I quietly answer back. "I usually park in an off-street garage, but I think I'll try to find a space in front."

"Why not put it in the garage? It will draw less attention."

"Good point, except I want to draw attention to the fact that we are in my apartment. That should keep all of the players in close proximity. Maybe the good guys and the bad guys will duke it out and we can sit and watch." I am trying to make light of a very questionable decision on my part, especially one that puts Liz at risk. Hell…she's a cop.

"If the good guys stake out your place, won't Billy get spooked?" I am not convinced Liz knows who the good guys are any more than I do.

"Maybe, but by leaving the Four Seasons, we've upset whatever plans that whomever has made." That mouthful of gobbledygook describes how I feel…or maybe how Billy feels. Don't trust anyone…anyone. "Liz, I think we trust each other. I am convinced that we are being played by others. I don't know the rules or even the game, but Billy is right, we've got to be very picky who we trust. The Four Seasons was lousy with cop types."

"And non-cop types," Detective Browne adds.

"Correct. So Billy needed to get us out of there and he pushed the buttons to do so. What bothers me is that it seems our teammates had a contingency plan ready to implement even as we were thinking about changing the first plan."

"Chris, you sound like a riddle."

"KISS."

"On the first date?" Liz starts to laugh again.

"KISS — keep it simple stupid. Our bosses figured we would change the plan. That's why they had surveillance teams in place. Remember, we weren't planning to leave until tomorrow morning."

"Meaning?"

"I'm not sure, but I don't like it. I don't see Captain Hancock in bed with either the CIA or the U.S. Attorney's Office."

"I feel the same way about Commander Marshall."

"There is no question that we are being set up. By whom? I'm clueless."

"To what end?" There is sharpness to Liz's voice.

"To get Billy. What I don't understand is why the elaborate charade if they want to assassinate him? I think they want to find out what he really knows."

"About the murders?"

"Liz, I think I have just experienced a deep and spiritual moment. The murders are the tip of the iceberg, metaphorically speaking. They need to ascertain what Billy knows about how the Feds are operating in the field."

"If I read between the lines," Detective Browne begins, "you are suggesting that the CIA may be operating domestically."

"I'm not suggesting it, I'm simply analyzing what Spinelli said this afternoon about the Agency's relationship with Billy."

"We are in deep shit!" Liz removes the little Browning from her pocketbook and slides the action, pushing a bullet into the chamber. "Chris, assume Billy knows that the CIA is carrying out covert domestic operations, including some in which he participated. Assume that the CIA wants him silenced but can't come out and say that. Assume that the FBI had Billy participate in some questionable activities as well and wants him silenced but can't come out and say that either. They get us to find Billy. Drop a few hints about Billy's allegiances with some bad folks, they get what they want, Billy and maybe you and me."

I almost rear-end the car in front of me.

"Liz, do you have any idea what you just said? It doesn't make sense."

"That's the problem, Chris. It makes perfect sense. Why

would the CIA and U.S. Attorney's office be in a meeting together, with us, discussing Billy O'Brien? They've got a common interest — him. And they're trying to cover up what he's been doing for them."

"But why us?"

"You were his best friend but you were a straight cop and locked him up. For what? A CIA hit? If you think about the crime scene, the evidence or lack thereof and most importantly the motive, you come up empty. We are their tools and we are therefore expendable."

"What you are talking about is a conspiracy that might spread from South Boston to the South Lawn. That's a lot to absorb."

"Chris, it doesn't fit otherwise. It's the only explanation."

"Time out! I need to think about this, especially in light of the participation of men we each respect and trust. I can't believe that Captain Hancock is involved in a cover up that makes Watergate look like a garden party. Shit!"

"Maybe I am over-reacting, but as far as I am concerned, there are too many unanswered questions. I have been following organized crime in Boston for almost my entire professional career and Billy O'Brien was a nothing until you collared him for a crime he probably didn't commit. Don't you think it a bit odd that no one did the most basic ballistic crosscheck?"

"As I keep saying, that's the difference between a street cop and a desk cop."

"Except for the fact, Mr. Street Cop, you didn't check the ballistics either."

"Make that ex-Mr. Street Cop and I didn't have access to the ballistic information nor the knowledge that the Feds had Billy on their payroll."

"Chris, did you find it strange that Billy never said a

thing about the murders?"

"If the assumption is that he was working for the Mob. It makes perfect sense. I've busted a number of low life types and they all believe in their bullshit Code of Silence."

"Do you think they believe it or are they afraid of what would happen to them and their familes if they break it?" Liz has a better handle on the psychological dynamics of Mob thought processes than I do.

"I need a minute and besides, we're here. Welcome to Chez Callahan, your convenient second floor walkup." I place the Chevy under the only streetlight on the block. I can't believe I even found a parking space, but then I remember that it is spring break and a lot of students who live in the 'hood are tanning themselves in faraway places for the week. I guess I'm entitled to a little good luck.

"How should we play this?" Liz asks. "Do we act as cops or lovers?"

"Is it an either/or question?" I look at Liz to gauge her reaction.

"Touché. Open my door, carry my bags and then I'll decide."

"Just keep the Browning handy."

"My thoughts exactly." I notice that the weapon is out of Liz's pocketbook. Cops first...maybe lovers later.

Simultaneously we each look in our respective side view mirrors. Nothing. I get out of the car, push the driver's door lock button and walk around the front of the car. I open the passenger's door, help Liz out of the car and try not to stare at her legs. I reach into the back seat, grab her shopping bags, push the door lock button and walk next to Liz, who puts her arm in mine.

"There's always tomorrow," she whispers.

CHAPTER TWENTY-THREE

"It's just a little too quiet," I whisper. "Those bozos who were following us have vanished. Hope they aren't calling for an airstrike."

"Quiet is better than noisy." Liz responds.

"I agree, especially gun-type noisy." We reach the front door and I put the key into the top lock and turn. Click.

"That's a good sign," I say, trying to sound confident.

"Explain." Detective Browne still has her revolver in her hand.

"It's a two-sided deadbolt. You need a key to turn the lock both entering and leaving. It's probably against code because you can't open the door in an emergency without the key, but I'll take the chance. Unless you are an expert burglar or have a duplicate key you can't relock the door, provided you were able to unlock it in the first place."

"I can't tell you how relieved I am." Liz sounds a bit sarcastic. "Please open the front door."

"I'm just trying to be efficient."

"Chris, I want to get into your apartment...now!"

I place the key in the other lock, turn it, and open the front door. "One flight up." Liz seems very uptight all of a sudden. Gun-in-hand, she climbs the stairs. Suddenly the light at the top of the stairs turns on. Liz drops to one knee.

"It's only a motion detector," I announce.

"Shit! It scared me half to death."

"That's why I should go first."

"But I have the gun."

"Which would be of no use if a real professional was waiting on the second floor landing."

"You're right, Chris. Sorry."

"No need to apologize."

At the top of the stairs I quickly step past Liz and start examining the door.

"Now what?" Liz's voice is definitely edgy.

"I want to check if I have had any uninvited guests in my apartment while I was gone." I run my hand along the door jam and find the several pieces of tape exactly where I had left them. "One can never be too careful."

"Okay?"

"Yes ma'am." I unlock the door and swing it open. Liz rushes in. I follow her and punch in the alarm code, close the door, and turn on the imitation-Tiffany lamp that proudly stands next to my faux-leather couch. All class.

"Where's the ladies' room?"

"Bathroom is down the hall. First door on the right. Light on the outside."

"Thanks." Liz tosses her baby Browning to me and sprints down the hall.

I grab the gun as deftly as I used to grab sinking line drives. I hope she put on the safety.

Liz returns and says, "Sorry, it was a matter of life and death. I didn't care if someone was waiting for us. I had to go." She smiles.

"Crisis averted. Can I show you around? It won't take

long."

"Now we've got all the time in the world."

I laugh. "First stop on the tour is the kitchen. Observe the stainless steel, six-burner stove with convection oven, Sub-Zero refrigerator with its own icemaker, filled with gourmet delicacies from every corner of the known world, a sink with disposal and a dishwasher."

"I feel like you're a real estate broker trying to sell me a condo." Liz once again places her arm in mine, which I am liking.

"I can't have you thinking Chris Callahan is an unsophisticated slob."

Liz leans over and kisses me lightly on the cheek. "Perish the thought."

"Perish is not a great choice of words," I reply.

This time Liz punches me in the shoulder. "Please continue the tour Mr. Sophisticate."

"As you can see, the floor plan in this unit is somewhat open."

"Does that explain the absence of furniture?"

"Ouch. You cut deeply."

"Actually, I spend a lot of time decorating. I specialize in cheap and cheerful."

"That explains it."

"Wait one minute. The leather on the couch might be fake, but the leather on each of those books is the real thing."

Floor to ceiling bookcases fill each of the interior walls. Liz walks around the room. Other than windows and a couple of old diplomas and citations, everything else is a book...well read...well-loved and many are rare first editions I have been collecting for years. When you have low overhead, you can afford to splurge on works of great literature.

"Chris, this is amazing. You've got some volumes that are incredible. A complete Audubon portfolio, a first edition copy of Washington Irving's Life of George Washington, Common Sense, complete works of Mark Twain. I can't believe it. Your collection must be worth a fortune."

"Books have always been my passion. Before the Internet, books were the only source of escape, of places and things and people in far-off places doing amazing things. The American experience has been written about by men and women of vision and talent and I wanted to read every book. I just didn't want to read a book once, I wanted to be able to pick it up again and again and find a pearl of wisdom that answered my question. Voilà! Twenty-plus years of yard sales, antique stores in Maine, small book dealers here in Cambridge and friends. It brings everything into perpective. However, we must deal with the balance of the tour and plan for...whatever."

"Lead on, MacDuff."

"Actually the quote is 'Lay on, MacDuff'."

"Have you always been such a pain in the ass?"

"Come to think about it...yes." What the hell, I give Liz a kiss, which to my relief, she does not resist. I apparove. I just hope we make it through the night.

"I know where the bathroom is and I'm not ready to see the bedroom, so let's make a plan. I just want to get through the night."

CHAPTER TWENTY-FOUR

"Chris? Now what?" Liz starts to pace, which in my apartment means living room to kitchen, about twenty feet, and back again.

"That's the $64,000 question. I've been asking myself, what is our overall objective?"

"That's been bothering me as well. Is it to deliver Billy to the Feds, who I don't think can be trusted?"

"Liz, if somehow we convince Billy to come in and talk, it's under the Captain's aegis. He gave his word."

Liz stops pacing and turns toward me. "You are a bit naïve, my charming friend. If the CIA wants Billy bad enough, Captain Hancock is powerless to do anything about it. He may be your King Arthur, but he is hardly at the top of the law enforcement food chain."

"Unfortunately, you are probably right. Then what the hell are we doing? We don't even know where to start."

"I think it is important to find out from Billy what went down, since it's obviously a big concern all around when witness protection is compromised. Having said that, until we actually make contact, the rest of our plan should remain fluid."

"Detective Browne, if I hear you correctly, the part

about bringing Billy in for interrogation is still up in the air. Correct?"

"You are wise beyond your years. I think we should concentrate on talking to Mr. O'Brien ourselves, before we go to phase two."

"Phase one is finding Billy. Phase two is talking to him and phase three is everything thereafter."

"I stand corrected, however, I am not changing from the basic premise that we need to formulate a plan independent of everyone else and find out what's going on."

"I'm retired, you're the one with a career on the line."

"My pension is the least of my concerns at this point. Frankly, I have a gut feeling that there is a piece of the puzzle that's missing. A large piece and I think that it has been intentionally withheld."

"By the Captain or Commander Marshall?"

"I sure as shit hope not, although it would make my decision to ignore the part about bringing in Billy a whole lot easier."

"Let's assume for the sake of argument that I agree with you. Have you thought about a strategy, other than waiting around, to get Billy to the surface?"

"Not really."

"Liz, that's not a big help. I am concerned that the so-called plan that Captain Hancock devised is totally dependent upon Billy wanting to talk and more importantly that I'm the guy he wants to listen. Although the notes at dinner are encouraging, no one has thought through how Billy is going to make face-to-face contact, assuming he wants to." I hate passivity and I feel like I'm watching a movie instead of participating.

"You're right. The present strategy, if you can call it

that, makes us totally passive, like spectators waiting for the next round." I close my eyes and slowly shake my head.

"What's wrong Chris?"

"I hope this comes out okay. Several times in the last ten minutes you have said exactly what I've been thinking. It's very creepy."

"Why?" Liz places her hands on my shoulders and begins massaging. "That feels good?"

"Well, it takes my mind off the task at hand and for another, I like it."

"Since we haven't agreed on the task at hand, no harm, no foul. And since when is feeling good such a bad thing?"

"It's hard to challenge irrefutable logic." I reach for Liz's hand and swing her around so that we are face to face. Her eyes close in anticipation. I opt for the face between the hands type kiss. I release her. "There's always tomorrow. Let's agree on the task at hand, shall we?"

"Chris Callahan...incurable romantic." Liz's smile lights up the room.

"It's the only disease that I hope has no cure." I touch Liz's hand. "However, we first need to figure out how to get Billy to come in out of the cold."

"Do you think he knows where we are?"

"I am going to make the following assumption. If the notes at the Four Seasons were from Billy, albeit delivered by go-betweens, then Billy saw us leave the restaurant and if he saw us leave, sooner or later, probably sooner, he'll come here. The car is outside on the street, my phone number is listed and we have enough lights on to indicate we are at home." Instinctively, I turn on another light.

"So, I gather you are suggesting we should simply hunker down and wait for him to knock on the door? Theoretically sound, but what about the goons who were following us and the fact that we don't know whether they were friend or foe."

"I think we also have to assume that everyone is a foe, even the so-called good guys."

"Chris, I've got a bad feeling. Do you think we are a target?"

"Not now, but I think we are dispensable, especially if we screw up someone else's plans."

"Or find out something certain people don't want to become common knowledge. Comforting thought."

I nod in reluctant agreement. "Liz, I have a few suggestions. First, I think you need to get out of that dress and into something more comfortable."

"Why Chris Callahan, if I didn't know better I might think you were trying to seduce me." Liz's voice assumes a definitely Southern lilt.

"And you'd be right, except that right now I want you to be in sweats and sneakers carrying something larger that your baby Browning."

"Ah shucks." We both begin to laugh. "I assume that's the bedroom?"

"Detective Browne, you've sleuthed out my boudoir."

"The No Trespassing sign is a dead giveaway." Liz picks up her shopping bags and sweeps into the bedroom. "No peeking!"

"Boy Scout's honor."

"Just make sure that you're always prepared." Making sure she gets in the last word, Liz closes the bedroom door behind her.

CHAPTER TWENTY-FIVE

Sitting across the kitchen table from Liz, both of us wearing rather dull gray sweats, sipping cups of Irish Breakfast tea, in the hopes that Billy O'Brien might drop in for a cuppa, makes me smile...inside. I don't want to tarnish the image, but I like domestication. Given the right set of circumstances, I would love to putter around in the yard, redecorate a room from time to time with treasures I've found at yard sales and even develop some serious culinary skills, using only herbs from my garden. Alas, this fantasy requires someone with whom I can share these pleasures. I think at this point in time, I'd be better served by finding Billy or should I say getting Billy to find me...us.

"You seem lost in thought, Chris," Liz observes.

"Trying to figure out the best way to implement phase one," I reply offhandedly.

"Unless my gut is wrong, Billy won't be able to get near this place without somebody grabbing him first. I am convinced that by now everyone knows where we are."

"And everybody is?" I ask.

"Our bosses, our colleagues, neither of whom I trust, and probably the folks that think Billy is or was one of their own."

"Are you implying that coming here wasn't a good idea?"

"Not at all. I don't think Billy could have done anything more than send you notes tonight at the Four Seasons. The place was lousy with cops and probably representatives of the Mob. Even if Billy had set up a rendezvous, we would have been followed. At least we're on your turf."

"If we had a dog, I'd suggest that we take him for a walk so that we'd be more visible."

"As long as it's not a pit bull. I admit to being prejudiced when it comes to dogs." Liz smiles. She probably assumes that guys like me want or possibly need, aggressive pets.

"I was thinking more in the Bichon Frise range. Small, cute, friendly and hypoallergenic." I'm not sure Liz believes me.

"You're kidding...right?"

"Actually, no. My mother's parents had a Bichon, who was with them for almost seventeen years. He was spoiled rotten, of course. I remember that even when he got older he was puppy-like. Whenever I'd sit down, he'd jump into my lap and fall asleep."

"Well, well, a deeply-hidden Callahan secret. You are a closet lapdog lover."

"Lest we digress too far, we still need to make it easier for Billy to contact us."

The first ring of the phone almost gave me a heart attack. The second ring made me look at Liz. I answered before the third ring.

"Callahan, here."

"Chris, what the hell are you doing home?" The voice shouts. I put my hand over the receiver and whisper to Liz, "Captain Hancock." She raises one eyebrow.

"And good evening to you too, sir." I pause and listen to his tirade.

"Captain, if I may explain. Your plan is flawed. Not for want of trying but because it depended on secrecy. There were more members of law enforcement at the Four Seasons than customers, with the possible exception of members of the Mob. Captain, your plan was leaked. By whom, I don't know. So, I improvised. I'm good at that... remember? I am going to fly solo until I straighten out a few things." I pause to listen to Captain Hancock sputtering something about the need to keep lines of communication open.

"Tell him I'm flying with you," Liz announces.

"Sir, Detective Browne wants you to know that she is staying with me as ordered...providing cover. This is my decision, not hers."

I place my hand over the receiver and whisper to Liz. "No point wasting a good pension."

"I want to get off the phone in case Billy tries to call. You've got to trust me. Detective Browne and I may go out for a walk in a few minutes. Have your people watch and see how many other people follow us. That should give you some sense of the cast of characters. Based on the cars in our motorcade to Cambridge, don't discount your friends at the FBI or Justice or CIA. I am going to do my best to meet with Billy, but I am not going to put myself or Detective Browne at more risk. This whole thing stinks. Good night, Captain." I breathe deeply.

"Wow," Liz starts, "I'll bet you've never spoken to him like that before."

"I've never worked for him before without him being my boss. It feels good."

"Chris, how much danger do you think we are really

in?" Her voice reflects both professionalism and fear.

"Personally, I think that we are absolutely safe until...if, Billy meets with us. Until then, we are the only link, albeit tenuous, to him. There are a number of folks who want to get their hands on him and I think that some of those folks are supposed to be on our side. I can only conclude that something or some things have gone down of which Billy has knowledge that very much compromises one or more of our colleagues. What we need to work out is whether it's personal or institutional."

"I'm not sure what you mean when you say personal or institutional?" Liz asks.

"We have to figure out if there is an Agency issue or possibly just a rogue agent issue. If there are policies about which we know nothing that are illegal, although always cloaked in national security rhetoric, that's one thing. If there is an individual or even a couple of people, who are making their own rules, that's altogether different." It's exhausting just pondering the different scenarios. What if more than one Agency, with or without the knowledge of the other, is engaging in illegal conduct and Billy was involved?

"Chris, I've been in law enforcement all my adult life. I believe in what I do and what those around me are doing...and how we are doing it. The rules have been bent... some maybe broken for too long...by too many. It was unacceptable and changes have been made. But you are raising the possibility that parts of the law enforcement community are still carrying on business in the old way."

"Liz, I think it's more than a possibility, more likely a probability, but not yet a fact. That's what we've got to figure out. The more I think about it, the more I convince myself that Billy is in more danger from us than he is from either himself or from the so-called bad guys. And what if the bad guys and the good guys are in cahoots?"

"Are you espousing a conspiracy theory?"

"Are you surprised?"

"I'm not sure how I feel about it. If there is a conspiracy, I don't want to be a part of it." Liz starts to pace again.

"A part of the conspiracy, I agree. But you have to be part of the cure."

"You, too."

"Maybe we need to reflect upon this with a glass of wine."

"Chris," Liz begins, "first things first."

"Yes?"

"I would like a couple of Tylenol, a glass of water and a quick walk around the block and then a glass of wine." Liz's smile once again lights up the room.

CHAPTER TWENTY-SIX

Fortunately my medicine cabinet, or rather the wicker basket in which everything pill-like resides, doesn't have a lot of occupants, so that locating a couple of Tylenol is quick work. My state-of-the-art Sub-Zero refrigerator has an ice/water dispenser, so I am able to provide the lovely Ms. Browne her pain relief in less than two minutes.

"Shit!" I shout when the phone once again makes me jump. This time I succeed in spilling an entire glass of water down the front of my sweatpants. In addition to my obvious embarrassment, the water is ice cold.

"Chris, you get the phone. I'll get the water." At least Liz doesn't start laughing at my accident. Her smile, which comes so easily, I can handle.

"Callahan," I answer.

"Skippy, don't say a word," the voice says.

Looking at Liz, I mouth the word Billy, pointing at the phone. She crosses the room, leans next to me, our heads separated only by the phone.

"Remember the city championship game against Dorchester? The final score of that game is the same as the final four digits of the number I want you to call from a pay phone. The first three digits are my mom's house address. Skippy…now!" The receiver clicks as Billy hangs up.

"Chris, what's going on?"

"That's the break we've been waiting for — Billy."

"Are you sure it was him?"

"Absolutely. No one else would call me by a name I haven't been called in twenty years and refer to an event that is important to no one except Billy and me."

"This is all good…right?"

"Not entirely."

"What are you talking about? Five minutes ago we were going to take a walk on the off chance that Billy would be hiding in some bushes and tell us to meet him somewhere secret. Now he calls with a contact number."

"Shit! I can't remember the score of the game. I haven't thought about it in decades and Billy wants me to call him back…now!"

"Chris, visualize the game just like it was yesterday. Let yourself drift back into your memory."

"It was right before Billy decided to borrow the priest's car. Our team was really good." My voice fades into my thoughts. I close my eyes. Why? Because that's how they do it on TV.

"Are you okay, Chris?" Liz's voice brings me back to reality.

"Got it! His mom's address — 721 P. Street and the game score was 11-10. 721-1110. We've got to get to a pay phone and call Billy.

"If there are any left." Liz's voice wakes me from my temporary euphoria. "We need a plan."

"We've got a plan. Call Billy."

"What about the folks lurking outside? They may be waiting to follow us or shoot us."

"Point made." I walk over to the front window and look out at the street. Not surprisingly, it looks like it did ten minutes ago...empty.

"Rather than risk being followed, call him on your cell," Liz suggests.

"Knowing Billy, he is probably watching us right now and is aware that we are being watched by both wise guys and cops. He wants us to be mobile. Being holed up here may be safe for us but it doesn't work for Billy."

"Can't you talk to him on the cell and set up a time and place to meet?"

"If we assume that my home phone is tapped, isn't it logical that they are also set up to hear my cell conversations? I'll bet that my cell has been bugged since the Captain called me this morning. I am beginning to feel that I...that we've been set up from the get go."

"Why?"

"There is something else going on. I feel it. Too many people with too many agendas." What I would really like to do is close my eyes and wish this whole damn thing away.

"How many ways out of this building?" Liz is all business.

"Front door, back door and a bulkhead to the basement," I reply.

"What about the roof?"

"We can access the roof easily. During the summer I have a container garden up there. Other than to throw a rope over the side and climb down, the roof is not an escape route."

A smile lights up Liz's face. "I presume you have rope. Correct?"

"You are certifiably crazy. It's cold, icy and it's a thirty-foot drop."

"Chris? Do you have a better plan?"

I stroke my chin. This is a crazy and dangerous idea. I need to think and talk at the same time. "I've got everything we need: a harness, heavy leather gloves and plenty of rope. I actually have done some serious climbing, which is why I think this is nuts."

I hope that Liz is not offended, but rappelling down the side of a house, in the cold and in the dark is definitely not a good plan.

"Let's pretend," I start, "that we have climbed down the side of the building without being seen, then what? We can't take my car since it is out front — under a streetlight. How do you suggest we get to where ever we are going?"

"You are right, which has led me to another idea I've been bouncing around."

"I hope it is better than the first. And less risky."

Liz rubs her chin, mocking me.

"Why not walk out the front door and get in your car and see who follows."

"And then what?"

"We'll cruise around until we find a payphone or maybe a couple of payphones. Assuming we have company, we stop and place a call to Billy. They won't be able to trace the call if it is under thirty seconds. We'll keep stopping and calling until you can make an arrangement with Billy to meet or determine that he's not going to talk. Each call lasting less than thirty seconds."

"Okay, then what?"

"As I recall, the Captain said you were good at improvising. At least you will know whether Billy is willing to go to the next level or not, which is a lot more knowledge than you have now."

"Your brilliance is only eclipsed by your beauty and

besides, I think your sweats are very sexy."

"Really?"

"They'll be even sexier after you put on a bulletproof vest."

"Why, Chris, you do care, don't you? Do you have the Armani tailored vest, the one with the cashmere lining."

"Sorry, all out. You'll have to settle for standard issue with a Nomex lining."

"Bulletproof and fireproof. How sweet." Liz walks across the room and without warning kisses me on the lips — hard."

"What do I get if I tell you my car is armor plated?"

"Well big boy, that all depends," Liz retorts.

"On what, my love?"

"On whether we make it to tomorrow. Let's get going. Billy awaits."

"Party pooper."

"Takes one to know one."

"My, my, aren't we being mature."

Liz kisses me again. Much softer. "Business first."

"The vest is in the closet in my bedroom. Your attire is unlikely to be affected. If I had known, I would have asked the Captain for some of that fancy body armor for you."

"We could wear them to bed — like matching pajamas."

She is way too distractive. "Back to business, Detective Browne. I think that I have an ankle holster for your baby Browning and you can tuck my spare Glock into your waist band."

Liz heads toward my bedroom. "No peeking, and tell me about Billy and the game."

"It's kind of a long story."

"Which you flashed through at light speed."

"I'll tell you in the car on the way to call him."

"And don't leave out any details."

"Sounds like you're writing an article for your high school paper"

"I just want all the facts."

"Yes, Sergeant Friday. Anything else?"

"Just go away. I'll be out in a second."

CHAPTER TWENTY-SEVEN

Looking a little like Tweedledee and Tweedledum in our almost-matching gray sweat suits, Liz and I casually walk out the front door of my building, hoping that we are not going to be greeted by a hail of bullets. So far, so good. Even with the bulletproof vest, Liz looks great.

Parking the car under a streetlight was both a good idea and a bad idea. The glow cast by the light reduces the shadows in which bad guys might lie and wait in ambush. However the light also makes us perfect targets.

"Maybe we should do some stretching exercises so that it looks like we are going for a late evening jog," Detective Browne suggests.

"Do you think it will throw them off our tail?"

"Your tail or mine?"

Suddenly, I feel a searing pain in my bicep.

"You are being a sexist pig," Liz announces to anyone within a block or two.

"I didn't know you could punch so hard," I reply rubbing my bruised arm.

"I won the Police Academy boxing championship in my weight class." Liz looks very pleased with herself. "The co-ed championship."

"But it hurts."

"You are a baby, but if it will make you feel better, I'll kiss it."

"Detective Browne, you have struck a fellow officer and you will be punished…severely."

"As I recall, you are retired and furthermore I didn't hit you as hard as I could have."

"Thanks for that piece of information. I'll remember it for the future." I certainly hope we have a future… preferably together. "Since we have been neither assaulted nor shot, I think we should execute plan A and see who follows."

Liz links her arm in mine and gives it a gentle kiss. It really doesn't hurt that much. "Chris, do we have a plan B?"

"But of course we have a plan B. We always have a plan B. I just haven't figured it out quite yet." I step back just in case Liz decides to hit me again.

"Open the car door. I'm freezing."

"Your wish is my command."

"As well it should, but I bet you say that to all the ladies."

"Only to lady cops and you are the only one I know." I lean over and give her a quick kiss, reach under the doorsill to see if the door has been opened in our absence, insert the key into the lock and open the door. "Buckle up."

"I guess that means no necking. What a waste of a bench seat."

I wonder if Liz is being so playful because she's scared. I don't blame her. I can't say that I feel real warm and fuzzy myself. I glance at my watch. I can't believe that it's only 10 p.m. Eight more hours until dawn. I walk around the front of the car, run my hand along the hood to see if it has been opened, repeat the sill check on the driver's side and open the door.

"Very thorough," Liz says professionally.

"It just wouldn't be any fun if someone decided to blow us up."

"OK fearless leader, where to?" Liz asks.

"I think we should try Mass. Ave. near Porter Square. There are a couple of convenience stores that might have pay phones and if all else fails, I am sure there are still some working units at the subway station."

"Chris, let's do some one-stop shopping." Liz is being entirely too obtuse for me.

"I think that all the stores on Newbury Street are closed."

Liz draws back her fist as if to hit me again.

"Do you want to listen or be a wise guy."

"Sorry." I lower my head in mock apology.

"There are five or six phones next to each other on the street-side wall of the MBTA station in Porter Square. Use one for thirty seconds and keep moving down the line."

"Very wise suggestion, provided that all the handsets are still connected to the phones and that there aren't other people using the phones."

"I guess we will just have to check it out and, as an added bonus, there's a Dunkin' Donut. I think I need a cup of coffee — black."

"Is that a suggestion or an order?" I ask.

"Consider it an impassioned off-hand remark," Liz responds.

"Yeah, sure. Admit it, you forgot your wallet and you want me to buy."

"True...true. You have found me out. I am an expensive date."

"You probably want a large, right?"

"I think this conversation has every possibility of spinning out of control, and a small will do. Regular. Thanks."

"You mean you want real sugar and real cream?"

"Consider it an investment."

"In what?"

"In me staying awake, so that I can cover your sorry butt."

"What does my butt have to be sorry for?"

Once again, I think we are bantering back and forth to avoid the next step. Starting the car, which hopefully will not ignite some kind of device that will launch us into space...in pieces. I don't want to telegraph my nervousness by hyperventilating. I turn the key. The sound of eight purring cylinders is music to my ears. I put the car into drive and head toward the lights and relative safety of Porter Square.

"Okay, it's story time about your baseball team. You promised." Liz sounds like a little kid. A very big little kid, but little kid nevertheless.

"Here goes. Once upon a time..." I wish I was sitting in front of a fire, snuggled up with Liz.

"Stop it Callahan! I want the real story."

"Our team was not the biggest, nor the fastest, but we played really well together. Billy was our spiritual leader and his uncle, Sean Malloy, was our coach. Uncle Sean had played for Southie in the early sixties and some said he was on a fast track for a professional career, maybe even the show. He was drafted into the Army within days after he graduated from high school and within three months was in Vietnam. Within a year, he was in a VA hospital with an artificial leg, compliments of a landmine. It didn't slow down Uncle Sean, but it did end his hopes for a big league career. He taught fundamental baseball. He drilled us for hours. He made us practice turning a double play or setting up a sacrifice bunt until we were perfect.

Billy was the ace of our pitching staff. Actually, Billy was our only real pitcher. I was his battery mate — the catcher. Unlike a lot of kids in their mid-teens, Billy never overthrew the ball. He never hurt his arm. He had superb control of his pitches. Actually, Billy had superb control of everything he did. I'm not boring you, am I?"

"I am interested, really. Please, keep going." I wonder if Liz is just humoring me. Getting my mind off...whatever it's on.

"I was just thinking that nobody picked up the signals about Billy's attitude. Billy was the toughest pitcher I ever caught, not mean. Actually, maybe mean is a good word. He would brush back a batter with inside fastballs as many times as was necessary to get him off the plate. If that didn't work, he hit him. He was good. It never looked like he was intentionally aiming at the batter; the ball just kind of got away from him." My voice begins to trail off again as I recall those days that seem a million years ago.

"Chris?"

"Just drifting off. Billy had pitched the day before in the semi-final game, he wasn't allowed to pitch in the championship game. Fortunately, Dorchester had also used their best pitcher in their semi-final game. Rather than give either team home advantage, the championship was held at Boston University, at Nickerson Field, built on site of the former Boston Braves stadium. The team left to go to Milwaukee in 1953, for which no one has forgiven them. Boston teams never move.

Without sounding like Howard Cosell, suffice it to say,

the game was a nail biter. Runs were being scored on great hits, great base running and remarkably...no errors. A lot of runs.

By a toss of the coin, Southie had been designated home team, so that we had the last at bats. Bottom of the seventh, which was the last inning, the score was 10-10. Ian Greene grounded out to third. I hit a line drive to right field which took a funny bounce in the outfield, which let me reach second. Are you sure you want to hear this?"

"I do want to hear the story and if I get bored I'll let you know. It was an important time in your life and I am interested. Okay Lieutenant Callahan?"

"But of course, Detective Browne."

"I hope this sweatshirt doesn't make me look like frumpy old detective."

"Not exactly." I brace for another punch.

"Please continue, sir."

"You asked for it. Mac was the next batter and lofted a fly ball to deep center, which was somehow caught. The good news was that the ball was hit so far, I tagged up and ran to third. Billy was the next batter. He used to choke up on the bat like the old-timers, Tris Speaker, Mel Ott and Ty Cobb, who was Billy's favorite player — naturally and the meanest man ever to play baseball. Billy could slap the ball anywhere for a single.

"You can't possibly be interested in this."

"Callahan, shut up and tell the story!" This time she did punch my arm, but not very hard.

"I was responsible for picking up the sign, but I couldn't figure out what Uncle Sean was signaling. I looked at Billy for some guidance. He just smiled at me...and winked. He stepped into the batter's box as a leftie. Billy was a right-handed batter. The first pitch was low and inside. Billy didn't move. Second pitch was high and inside. Billy didn't move. The next pitch was either going to hit him or be a strike across the plate. The pitcher wound up and Billy squared around to bunt. A sacrifice? No way, there were two outs. It was a squeeze play. I start toward home as fast as I can. Billy lay down a perfect drag bunt pushing the ball toward a completely dumbfounded first baseman. I did a belly flop slide and Billy safely reached first. We won 11-10!'"

CHAPTER TWENTY-EIGHT

One of the advantages of having no idea what you are doing is that those folks who may be following you or otherwise trying to disrupt your plans are simply out of luck. You can't disrupt a plan that doesn't exist.

Porter Square is the stepsister of Harvard Square and the big brother of Davis Square, which is actually in Somerville, but the next stop on the T. Many of the small specialty shops and non-chain restaurants that once dotted the Harvard Square landscape have been forced to migrate up Massachusetts Avenue to find more affordable rents. The same is true with a lot of old-time residents and faculty members who simply can no longer afford the cost of real estate near Harvard. Since the T's Red Line, along with surface buses, links the squares, the stigma of living in Porter Square is fading.

"Keep your eyes open for a parking space," I ask Liz.

"You can double park and I'll wait in the car."

"No way am I letting you out of my sight."

"Should I feel flattered or scared?"

"Both. Liz, I don't have any clue what is going on, but I want to keep you near me."

"Because of my charm, good looks or because I am

carrying a lot of firepower?"

"All three."

"Callahan, did anyone ever say that you are a charmer?"

"Does my mother count?"

"Of course your mother counts, but I suspect that she might have called you a charmer for entirely different reasons." Liz unfastens her seat belt, slides along the vinyl bench seat and puts her arm over my shoulder. "Keep your eyes on the road and your hands on the wheel."

"You are being unfair."

"Correct. I always play unfairly." Liz kisses me on the cheek.

"How am I supposed to concentrate?"

"On what?"

"Good point. Let's look for a parking space, make whatever phone calls are required and get an ice cream cone."

"It's only 30 degrees outside."

"We can eat the ice cream...inside. How's that for logic, Detective Browne?"

"After you've made the phone calls, I have a sneaking suspicion that we will be off on a snipe hunt."

"I haven't heard anyone use that expression in years."

"Guess I am not as young as I look."

"Fishing for a compliment, are we?" I sneak a glance at Liz.

"It's a woman's prerogative."

"Consider yourself complimented."

"Chris! Over there!"

"What?" I instinctively reach into my waistband.

"A parking space."

I hope the sound of my heart beating about 200 times per minute is not heard by Liz. It doesn't inspire confidence.

"I see it. Next time we look for a parking space, just point, don't shout, especially if there is a possibility that someone is following us. I almost had a heart attack."

"Sorry. Should I go back to my side of the front seat?"

"I prefer us both in the back seat."

"Now, now Mr. Callahan, I'm not sure how to take that remark. We are professional colleagues, working on a case."

"Undercover...remember?"

"Undercover does not mean under the covers."

"I don't think you've read the manual on clandestine operations, yet."

"Does that give you license to make suggestive remarks?"

"Yup."

"Good, I just wanted to get that straight." Liz gives me a quick kiss and slides over to the passenger side of my trusty Chevy.

Parallel parking without power steering can be a challenge, but working out in the gym several times a week has prepared me. The added pressure of Liz watching brings a drop of sweat to my brow. Yes! Perfect — six inches from the curb. Any driving instructor would be proud to have such a student.

"Please leadeth to the phones fair lady," I say while opening Liz's door.

"Shakespeare?"

"Callahan."

"But, of course." Liz hooks her arm in mine and we cross Mass. Ave. very carefully since we are crossing against the light and in the middle of the block. Gotta love it.

CHAPTER TWENTY-NINE

It never ceases to amaze me that there are still payphones, let alone four in a row — un-vandalized. Of course, none is being used, although I see that there are at least thirty people walking and talking on their cell phones and about an equal number texting. I'm okay with technology, it's just that it has replaced human skills and in some people, intimacy. For example, why text when you can talk? Say what you want to say, listen to the other person and that's that. It is now so out of control that special legislation is required prohibiting texting while driving. It's hard enough to drive a car in a place like Boston without constantly looking at a six-square-inch screen.

"Are you still on this planet Mr. Callahan?" Liz rudely interrupts my deeply-advanced thought processes.

"Just gathering up some additional courage," I reply. I reach into my pocket and pull out several quarters, dimes and nickels and approach the phone farthest from the subway entrance, which is probably counter-intuitive since if something goes wrong I could dash into the crowded subway and escape. It always works in movies.

"Chris?" Detective Browne is getting impatient.

I remove the receiver, insert a quarter and a dime for

what I hope will be less than a thirty-second phone call and punch in the numbers that I hope are right. After two rings I hear, "Skippy, be careful. You are in over your head. Call this number again in ten minutes. Get an ice cream." The phone call ends.

"Knock, knock." Liz taps the wall next to the phone.

"It was Billy. He told me to be careful, to get an ice cream and call him back in ten minutes."

"Did he tell you what kind?"

"What?"

"Of ice cream. Sorry, just trying to make a little joke. I am getting very spooked."

"Is that a professional term?"

"Actually when you are weak in the knees and you are short of breath and petrified, it's called being spooked."

"Got it. What kind of ice cream do you want?"

"Rum raisin with extra rum."

"Point well taken, Detective Browne. Let's walk over to Brigham's just in case someone is watching us."

"At least there are other people around."

"All having ice cream. It's a New England tradition."

"Seriously Chris, what is your take on all this?"

"I am beginning to give credibility to a conspiracy theory which goes something like this. Billy has been in deep cover for a long time, but for whom? While the CIA would appeal to Billy's sense of action, adventure and romance à la James Bond, I can't figure how they would have identified and then recruited him. He was a local kid in trouble, not some high-profile type. So I am thinking that Spinelli lined up Billy when he was on the force and pushed him over to the CIA and followed shortly thereafter."

"I can't say it isn't possible. Actually it makes sense. The CIA doesn't trust the FBI on the domestic side, so it hires some independent contractors and what better cover than being associated with the Mob? I think I would have gotten some hint that he was on board."

"Maybe, but let's not rule it out."

"Are you sure that your own Department wasn't involved, other than Spinelli? And why him?" Liz is not leaving any stone untouched.

"Pete was always a climber and he wasn't going to climb fast enough or high enough in the Boston Police Department. It wouldn't surprise me if he wasn't a mole for the Agency."

"Keeping them informed of goings on."

"It seems likely. Basically we've got every branch of law enforcement, foreign and domestic, as a possible participant. Doesn't narrow down the field much."

"Chris, I am troubled by the very scope of the involvement of all the good guys. Assume Billy was working for Spinelli, did he work for Feinstein's people independently or as an employee of the CIA?"

"Food for thought. Try this on for size. Maybe Billy was really a member of the Family all along and was penetrating both the CIA and FBI on their behalf?"

"Why are we talking about organized crime and terrorism at the same time?"

"Aren't they mutually exclusive?"

"Traditionally, they were mutually exclusive. Organized crime was very patriotic. Proud to be Americans. The scenario that the Families were somehow mixed up with terrorism does not fit."

"Detective Browne, try this on for size. The Mob of old is being pushed out of the drug trade by Mexicans, out of muscle business by Asian gangs and out of money laundering by Arabs, none of whom give a damn about

Old Glory. Unfortunately, none of this remotely helps explain Billy's role in this mess. Shit! I've got to call again."

CHAPTER THIRTY

I race back to the phones. Take a deep breath and dial Billy's number. One ring...two rings...three rings...shit! No answer. I feel the presence of someone next to me and it is not Liz.

"Skippy, just listen. Don't hang up. Pretend you are talking to someone. There are forces at work that you don't understand. Forces of good are doing evil and evil is doing more evil. If you hear that something has happened to me, act appropriately sad and wait for me to contact you."

"Are you a good guy or a bad guy, Billy?"

"Altar boy good. Later."

I slowly turn around and see no one...except Liz who is walking toward me holding two ice cream cones.

"Chris, you look like you've just seen a ghost. Are you okay? Did you reach Billy? Chris...Chris."

"He didn't answer the phone."

"Do you have any idea why?"

I nod. "Because he was here," I point at my feet, "and he spoke to me. Give me a minute to think this out."

"Chris, let's act nonchalantly in case someone is watching. I thought you were the mint chocolate chip type." Liz proffers a cone. "I think we should eat our cones, get into your car, go back to your apartment and talk."

"Good plan, madam detective. Good plan."

I am in such a state of shock that I am surprised that I can actually taste the ice cream. It's good. Brigham's is a Boston icon, synonymous with ice cream. It's like comfort food, but cold.

"Chris, there are a couple of people standing around your car." I was so engaged in ice cream licking that I hadn't noticed.

"Shall we casually join them?"

"With heat?"

"Just don't melt the ice cream."

Liz smiles, but reaches into the waistband of her sweats. The group doesn't look menacing, just motor heads discussing what might lie underneath the hood of the Chevy.

"Hey mister. These your wheels?"

I nod.

Another asks, "Is it a 305 or a 327?"

"Actually, it's a 350, bored, stroked and balanced with a high-rise manifold, four-barrel carb and headers."

"Great wheels," the first kid says. "Very cool. Thanks."

The group heads across the street. I hear the first kid say, I told you it was a sleeper.

"Nervous?" Liz takes a huge lick of her cone.

"Nah, none of them was packing anything more dangerous than cigarettes." I smile.

"Let's go home." Funny how Liz referred to my apartment as home. Maybe I am reading too much into it. I unlock her door and open it. She hands me her partially-eaten cone. "Would you mind throwing the rest away?"

"Being a bit intimate, aren't we?"

"If the going gets tough — "

"The tough go to Brigham's." I dump what remains of our ice cream cones into a trashcan.

I start the car, fasten my seat belt and instinctively look into the rearview mirror. Nothing. I don't know whether to take that as a good sign or a bad sign. I retrace our route so that anyone who might be interested wouldn't have any difficulty following us. I again check the mirrors. Still no sign of company. I opt to park the car in its rightful spot.

We briskly walk from the garage to my house, as much because we are getting cold as the inherent unknown risk factor. I decide that since we left by the front door, returning the same way makes us less conspicuous, albeit a potentially greater target. Somehow, I don't think anyone is interested in us, at least not yet. I guess that assumes no one knows I made contact with Billy. As before, I unlock the double bolt, I check my makeshift tape tell-tales, unlock the apartment door and punch in the code for the alarm system. And, as before, no one has been in my apartment. Curious. But then I remember that parabolic microphones and other sophisticated listening devices that now make physical entry into a unit unnecessary if all you want to do is hear what's going on inside.

"Chris, what are you doing?"

"I am turning on music...of sorts." I power up a devise that looks like a Bose receiver but emits a very high frequency sound designed to disrupt those same very sophisticated listening devices. SuperSpy magazine has a great classified ad section from which black-marketed, high-tech equipment is sold to every third-world country... and every second-rate ex-cop.

"Let's talk." I walk over to Liz.

"In a minute." She gives me one serious kiss.

CHAPTER THIRTY-ONE

I debate whether kissing is more important than telling Liz what Billy said. With trepidation, I opt for the latter since once this mess is over, there will be plenty of time for kissing, I hope.

"I need a glass of wine," Liz says, anticipating my suggestion by a microsecond.

"Red or white? More specifically a 2000 Château Pichon or a 2008 Chardonnay from the Central Coast in Napa?"

"I think we should save the Bordeaux for a special occasion —"

"Like survival," I quip.

"That's not the way I would have said it, but survival works. Speaking of which, what did Billy say?"

"I was wondering when you'd ask."

"And I was wondering when you'd tell me."

"Basically, he confirmed that there is something very rotten in Denmark or Boston in this case. Billy is reasonably sure that someone wants to do him in."

"Targeted?"

"He said that he thought something was going to happen to him, but not really."

"That is about as clear as mud, Mr. Callahan."

"Liz, he said I should act saddened at news, which I assume to be his death, but that he'd get in touch later."

"Sounds like he is trying to create some maneuvering space." Liz is probably right. Billy is trying to take some heat off himself and/or maybe us as well.

"Probably," I mutter. "He said something else."

"What?"

"That he still values our friendship."

"Since the only thing for us to do is to wait until Billy contacts us, let's open the Chardonnay and try to relax."

"Callahan's third rule." I hold up three fingers.

"What?"

"Never drink with a beautiful woman, especially if she's s cop, if she's packing heat." Liz's laugh is infectious. She hands me the Glock from her waistband and then slowly removes the ankle holster with her Browning. She places both on the table — still within reach. I hope she's not planning to use them if I get too fresh.

"Close your eyes," she demands. I do...sort of.

Liz pulls the baggy sweatshirt over her head, removes the body armor, runs her hands through her hair and starts to tickle me, wearing only a tank top and ugly sweatpants.

"I give up." I raise my hands to surrender. I'm not really ticklish, but hopefully it serves to relieve the tension.

"Detective Browne's third rule." She holds up three fingers. "Never drink wine with a man unless you each have on the same amount of clothing." She tugs my sweatshirt.

"Okay, okay, but you don't have to close your eyes."

"Like yours were closed?"

I tug off my sweatshirt, body armor and place my weapons next to Liz's.

Despite being freezing outside and chilly inside because

I forgot to turn up the thermostat when we returned, sitting around in a tee-shirt and sweatpants with Liz is pleasantly warm.

"I'll open the wine."

"I'm actually going to change into something a bit more comfortable," Liz announces.

Wait a minute, I thought she only had what was in the shopping bags, basically her sweat suit and her dress. I shrug, shake my head once and walk over to the Sub-Zero. One of my favorite things that I bought for myself is a large, counter-mounted French wine opener. Place the bottle between two short arms, pull the handle into the cork and raise the handle. Voilà. It even works with the new fake corks, which are made of a kind of plastic. I remove two appropriately shaped wine glasses from the cupboard and return to the living room.

"Very chic, don't you agree?" I almost drop the glasses. Liz is wearing, as best as I can tell, my XXL rugby shirt... period.

In a desperate attempt to recover from my obvious shock, I say, "My, my, don't you look stunning in blue and orange stripes."

"Care to pour me a glass of wine?"

"Oui, but of course, mademoiselle." As deftly as possible, while trying not to stare at Liz, I place the two glasses on the table in front of the couch, ignore the pile of guns and pour the properly-chilled Chardonnay. I proffer a glass to Detective Browne, pick up the remaining chalice and say, "Cheers!"

"Chris, thanks."

"For what?" I don't want to sound too stupid but I am clueless.

"For being you."

"Liz, I think you are paying me a compliment, but I am not sure what I have done to deserve it."

"Think about it, everything you've done is because you believe it is the right thing to do. You got roped into this fiasco, although you could easily have said no thanks, but you didn't."

"Lucky me." I twirl my finger.

"Shut up Callahan, I've got something to say. You care. You care about people, even a guy who you thought was a double murderer. You aren't afraid to say what you think and act on your beliefs and despite what you might see on television, that kind of person is rare and I for one think you are terrific."

I return my glass to the table, walk over to Liz and give her the biggest, but gentlest, hug I can. "Thanks. I'm not sure what to say, but thanks." I follow the hug with a kiss.

"Say nothing." Liz returns my kiss.

I can hardly believe this. Here I am with a gorgeous, bright and sensitive cop, who is wearing only a rugby shirt, in my living room.

"Chris," she whispers.

"Yes?"

"This doesn't mean I'm going to sleep with you tonight, it means that there will be other nights, I hope."

Surprisingly, I don't feel that was a put down. "We're still on duty…more or less."

"I would hate it if we were disturbed in the middle of the night." Liz smells good despite the fact that we've been on the go all day.

"There's always tomorrow." It's the only reply that comes to mind.

"There's also tonight." Liz lifts her glass. I retrieve my glass and we clink. I am strangely relieved at Liz's comments, since being interrupted at an inopportune time would be worse than deferring for a little while.

"I wonder who will call us first; Billy or someone telling us Billy is dead?" Until I…we get to the bottom of whatever is going on, deferral is definitely the best policy.

"Would you like me to make something to eat?" Liz asks.

"I think the larder is full and if we are going to keep our wits about us and drink wine at the same time, maybe a little something to eat, other than ice cream, is probably a good idea." I finally take a sip of the Chardonnay. Not bad. Not too oaky, dry with a nice citrus nose.

CHAPTER THIRTY-TWO

We work in the kitchen in silence, reacting to each other's movements in the rather cramped cooking quarters. Twenty minutes later, violà, pasta alla carbonara. We use fettuccine rather than spaghetti, both Pecorino and Parmesan cheese, egg yolks and pancetta. Liz suggests adding some peas for color. During the preparation process we used a little wine for the pasta, but the balance for ourselves. I think it is fair to assume that whatever else happens in the Billy O'Brien case will simply have to wait until tomorrow since it's almost midnight. We opt to sit in the living room rather than at either the breakfast nook or dining room table, which is covered with mail and magazines, all destined for recycling. It's times like these when I wish I had installed a gas-burning fireplace.

"This is really good. I didn't realize how hungry I was."

"Working in the kitchen with you seemed so natural. I instinctively knew where everything was. Chris?" Liz's voice trails off.

"Let's enjoy the food, the wine and each other's company. Then, if I may be so bold as to suggest we go to bed…each in a separate room."

"Can't we snuggle together?"

"I may not be able to resist temptation."

"Try real hard."

I lift my fork in a false salute. "Real hard."

"Don't be fresh. Eat." Liz twirls her fork into the unsuspecting pasta.

Clearly Detective Browne was as hungry as I was. Within ten minutes we are both members of the clean plate club. I rise and say, "I'll do the dishes."

"Here's the deal Callahan — you wash, I dry."

"Sounds like a plan."

"Speaking of which, did Billy give any indication when he was going to die?"

"The only sense I got was that it was imminent."

We make short work of the dishes.

"Chris, I think we should turn in. I get the bathroom first."

"Great, I can watch the Late Night Show." Without warning, Liz hits me again. "Are you going to make a habit of beating on me?"

"Only if the circumstances warrant. I need to keep you in line." She gives me another kiss on the cheek. "Garlic. I need to brush my teeth."

I watch her glide toward the bathroom. I admit that I am a dirty old man…maybe not so old. I wish I hadn't promised to be good. I am shaken out of my lechery by the ringing of the phone. It's almost one in the morning.

"Callahan."

"Chris, Pete Spinelli. I just got word that Billy's body was fished out of the Charles River about twenty minutes ago. Not pretty. Typical Mob hit. Hands and tongue cut off and his face was messed up pretty bad."

I take a deep breath. "How do you know it's Billy?"

"Remember that religious medal he always wore? It

was around the neck of the body. And Billy would never part with the medal."

"It was his grandfather's. He was killed by the British during the Easter uprising in 1916. You're right, Billy would never part with that. Shit. Part of me wishes I could have met with him to find out what went down. The other part is happy that this is over."

"Amen. I'm sure the Captain will want to meet sometime tomorrow. Someone will let you know before nine. Get some sleep. Oh...is Detective Browne still with you?"

"Of course, we were told to stay together." I hear a rather disgusting snort on the other end of the line.

"Sorry. Someone just came into the office."

"Right." I try not to sound too unbelieving. It's after midnight and he's in the office? Why? "When you hear the details about the funeral and wake, please let me know."

"Sure thing, Chris. Talk to you in the morning." Again I hear that snort. I hang up before I say anything I might regret.

"Who was that?" I am totally oblivious to the fact that Liz is standing next to me.

"Our esteemed colleague from the CIA, reporting that Billy's body was found in the Charles. It was a mob job, according to Pete."

"And?"

"We wait for Billy's call. Might as well get some sleep."

Liz reaches for my hand and pulls me toward the bedroom. It's my turn to use the bathroom. She starts to laugh.

CHAPTER THIRTY-THREE

My promise to Liz to limit our nighttime activities to snuggling was meaningless. Within about thirty seconds of our respective heads hitting the pillows, we were both sound asleep. The phone didn't ring until after seven the next morning. It took a second for me to become aware of the fact that it was really the phone, not a dream. Panic sets in. What if I don't answer the phone before the caller hangs up.

"Chris, it's the phone!"

"I know," I reply, grabbing the receiver from under my bed.

"Callahan." My voice sounds like a frog.

"Tough night, Skippy? How long did it take for them to discover my body? They called you, didn't they?"

"Yeah, Spinelli. It was almost one. He said he was in his office. I didn't check caller ID, but what the hell is he doing in his office?"

"Surprised? Don't be. Meet me at IHOP at the end of Soldier's Field Road in twenty minutes. Ask to sit in booth 13. My lucky number. Bring along the lady."

"Billy?" Liz pokes me in the shoulder to be sure I'm paying attention.

"None other. Quick resurrection. He wants us to meet

him in twenty minutes."

"No way! I've got to shower and fix my hair."

"Better start now. Clean towels are in the linen closet. I'll put on some water for tea."

"Do you have a hair drier at least?"

"As a matter of fact, yes. Under the sink."

"What time is it?" Liz is as disoriented as I am.

"A little after seven."

"I crashed last night. Sorry."

"So did I and don't be."

"Don't be what?"

"Sorry." I lean over and give her a quick kiss, spin her around and lightly push her toward the door. "Hurry Detective Browne, crime waits for no one's hair."

"Wrong. It always waited for Farrah."

"True, but you are no Angel."

"And you're not Charlie." Once again Liz punches me in the arm, but not as hard as before.

Detective Browne cleans up pretty good in fifteen minutes, giving me one minute to get ready. I choose to leave the stubble but brush the teeth. "Let's go."

"Do you think we're being watched?"

"I suspect that Billy's death is already common knowledge and that there are a whole lot of folks who are breathing a sigh of relief. As long as he remains dead, we are of no consequence to anyone. Did I tell you Spinelli wants to schedule a post mortem meeting for later today?"

"I hope we can get a better handle on what is going on from Billy. Where are we meeting him?"

"IHOP."

"Good, I'm hungry."

Again, looking like rejects from the YMCA, we retrace our steps to my car. For this excursion, I have opted for the ankle holster with the .38, while Liz drops her pea shooter into a small canvas purse-like tote bag with 02138 stenciled on the front.

"Clever pocketbook concept," I remark.

"They're cute. You can get different zip codes, so everyone knows where you are from."

"It's perfect for the lady on the go, especially the lady with a small but lethal automatic."

The garage door opens without incident and I quickly back the Chevy out onto the street. Because it's spring break, there is very little traffic until we get to Soldier's Field Road, which is kind of an extension of Storrow Drive. It runs along the river on the Boston side. We head outbound toward Brighton.

The International House of Pancakes franchise never ceases to amaze me. Despite the national obsession with healthier eating, weight and image, the instant you enter any IHOP, you find piles of pancakes, pounds of butter and gallons of imitation maple syrup. But it does taste great.

The parking lot is about half full. No obvious unmarked cars or Lincoln Town cars with blackened windows. Maybe Billy's choice of a venue was a good idea. I have so many questions and so few answers.

"May we be seated at table thirteen?" I ask the hostess.

"Certainly, sir," she replies as if she had been waiting for us. "Coffee?"

"I'd like some. How about you, Chris?"

"May I have a large orange juice to start?"

"Certainly. Your server will be here in a minute."

IHOP has about the largest menus I have ever seen. A kid can get lost behind one. I hand the eight-page, oversized, plastic-covered tome to Liz.

Suddenly, we hear a voice coming from the remaining menu.

"Good morning and welcome to the International House of Pancakes and crooks on the run." Billy sounds pleased with himself. "I planted this two-way microphone so that we can talk while you pretend to be talking to Ms. Browne."

"How'd you know my name?" Liz is sputtering.

"Please keep eye contact with Skippy...Chris. I will explain everything as simply and as quickly as a very complicated and lengthy story requires. Let me start by saying that I am sorry you got sucked into this mess and more importantly, Skippy, I am sorry that in order to do what I had to do, I lost you as a friend. I hope to remedy that. To put your collective minds to rest, I have never killed anyone. I haven't even broken any arms. After a couple of weeks in JD hall, I realized that I was a complete jerk. I wasn't like those other kids. I was angry, but at myself, not the world or my old man. I was lucky. Before I could do myself any real damage a counselor got me to focus on who I was and what I could do for others. Cletus, that was the counselor's name, hooked me up with Captain Hancock, and I became his eyes and ears. He got me into Harvard. I did very well, but I had to remain in deep cover."

"Have you decided what you'd like to order?" Both Liz and I are snapped out of our trance. A rather plump, dyed redhead with the brightest blue eyes I have ever seen, is hovering over us.

"May we have a minute?" Liz recovers faster than I.

"Of course, sweetie, take all the time you need." The waitress retreats to another table.

"Billy, how did you know to stop talking?"

"Don't look, but in addition to the microphones,

there are two micro cameras aimed at you and the lovely Detective Browne," Billy replies.

"Call me Liz. All my friends do."

"I am flattered to be a part of that select group."

"Can we cut the small talk? What the hell is going on?" I feel the first drop of sweat running down my spine.

"When Spinelli left the force, he asked Captain Hancock if he could take me to the CIA. Spinelli, to the best of my knowledge is straight. He is strictly a company man. So I got traded without the benefit of free agency and started working for the CIA. All I did was observe and report. As you well know, Liz, the Families have all but lost control of organized crime. Drugs, enforcement, money-laundering…you name it. The Agency was trying to trace terrorist financing. What emerged was very ugly. Actually, a form of home grown terrorism. There are American born-and-bred crazies who are fighting their own jihad. The face of these good old boys is not limited to the South or the West, but can be found amongst the urban un- and under-employed. Basically anyone, provided they are white and Christian, who feel their lot in life is caused by others, including Afro-Americans, Latinos, Asians, gays and of course, Jews. Muslims have been added to the list over the last decade or so. Recently, the ranks of the right fringe have swelled with middle class or former middle class folks who have been badly hurt in this economy. They are not profiled because they look like everyone else. They are dangerous. They want Constitutional rights even if it means taking away Constitutional protections."

"Billy, how do you fit into this?" Liz is trying to remove the soapbox from under Billy's feet.

"As you are undoubtedly aware, the CIA and the FBI do not take one another into their confidence, despite

9/11. In the course of following the money, what emerged is a pattern of Middle East money falling into the hands of American extremists, which at first didn't make sense."

"I thought you said this group puts Muslims on their shit list." I just wanted to show that I was still awake.

"Exactly! The Agency's ability to trace the money is limited by their scope of operation. So the Agency asked the FBI to continue following the money. The Bureau drags its feet because they have their own agenda regarding the crazies."

"Why?" Liz asks. "Wait a second, we need to order."

CHAPTER THIRTY-FOUR

"Ready yet?" The waitress has a bit of an edge to her voice since we've been sitting for twenty minutes taking up space.

"May I have a short stack of blueberry pancakes with bacon?" I guess our discussions with Billy have given Liz an appetite.

"And you, sir?" I detect a bit of surliness.

"Western omelet, wheat toast, well-done home fries and a cup of tea...please."

At least Miss Personality doesn't lick the end of her pencil when she writes down our order.

"No fair," Billy's voice returns to the conversation. "I'm getting hungry, too."

"No you aren't," I say. "Because you're dead."

"Skippy, that hurt. Liz, to answer your question, I think that there are a lot of people in the Bureau who sympathize with the crazies. Just look at the immigration issue. I want to continue with background." Billy sounds like he is sitting right next to us.

"I stayed in cover and kept in touch with Spinelli from time-to-time, but there wasn't a lot going on. About eighteen months ago, I was asked to drive someone important to a meeting. Sorry Liz, I don't want to talk names just now. Anyway, it was a meeting between several members of the Family and a group made up of representatives from several Mexican drug cartels. The ones who are killing each other every day. I placed a couple of micro bugs on my employers and what I heard was unbelievable. First, I never imagined that opposing drug factions would sit at the same table, but then again, it's the same as several Families sitting down to divide up things. Bottom line, the Family wants the Mexicans to help them get back the protection business from the gooks, their word, not mine. In exchange, they'll leave the drugs to the Mexicans."

"Wish I had heard that conversation," Liz says. "I had no idea."

"Billy, our food is coming. Shall I feed the microphone a few home fries?"

Actually, our breakfast looks and smells very good. Liz and I dig in as Billy continues.

"Thanks, pal. Spinelli is going nuts. First, money from the Middle East and now the Mob and the Mexicans. The two seem incongruent and here's the interesting part…"

"Trust me Billy," I say shoveling eggs into my mouth, "It's all interesting. It's just that it isn't hanging together."

"What if I told you that the heads of the Families, who we all think talk and look like the Sopranos, are smarter and tougher than we give them credit for."

"Explain, Billy. Of late, the Mob is being headed by an increasingly elderly group of men — "

"Who all have sons with Harvard Business School degrees." Billy interrupts. "They just appear respectable and not involved. Coupled with the fact that the economy has made it easier to recruit muscle, the Families are more formidable than they have been in years…decades."

"I have been involved with the activities of organized crime for a long time and all this is news to me. What happened to inter law enforcement cooperation?" Liz is hopping mad.

"You weren't supposed to know. The Agency decided that it simply couldn't rely on the FBI, which translates that neither state nor local law enforcement got this information."

"Go back to the connection between the money and the drugs." I think there must be a connection. What it is, I cannot fathom.

"The Families don't really want to give up the drugs to the Mexicans or to anybody. So, who are the sworn enemies of the Mexicans?"

"Shit! The fuckin' crazies." I hope I'm not shouting.

"Bingo."

"The Dons and the crazies, who would have imagined? But there are two big pieces missing. First, the Asians and second, the money laundering."

"Keep it simple, Skippy. Let the Mexicans put some serious muscle on the Asian gangs here on the East Coast, where they are less established and less organized. Leave the West alone. Once their presence is re-established in the protection business, the Mob only has to nudge the crazies into a large-scale war with the Mexicans all along the border."

"Financed by the Middle East? That's where I don't follow you," Liz says.

"Don't try to connect all the dots. The purpose of the Middle Eastern money to the crazies is just to keep the water boiling. It's like bomb threats where the bomb is actually a fake. It's disruptive. The crazies are a disruptive influence. Keep America on edge. Keep us guessing — distracted. It is the first principal of terrorism."

"Billy, this is very scary. I don't know what else to say. It is fuckin' very scary."

"We need to unravel a couple of things." I sense that Liz is willing to go just so far. "What is your involvement in this conspiracy of silence? More importantly, what is the involvement of the other law enforcement agencies, especially the CIA who seem to have a domestic agenda?"

"Is there another time and place to discuss this? I think we are being a bit conspicuous." Instinct or paranoia? It really doesn't matter. We've worn out our welcome. There is a line at the hostess station waiting to be seated…and we are probably making too much noise anyway.

"Skippy, you're right, as always, the voice of reason. I need to set something up. I will call your cell in an hour. To be continued. Adieu."

CHAPTER THIRTY-FIVE

"Now, what?" Liz asks the obvious.

"We wait an hour for Billy to call."

"Since we have time to kill, no pun intended, can you take me home so that I can get a change of clothes?"

"Where's home?"

"Where the heart is."

"Then I guess we should go back to my apartment."

"Later. First, we go to where the clean clothes are."

"Should I guess where to drive or will you give me a hint?"

"Sorry, Chestnut Hill Avenue at Comm. Ave."

I decide to go back down Soldier's Field Road and bear right toward Western Ave. It only takes about ten minutes to get to Liz's apartment building, a late-19th century, gray granite, six-story building that looks as if it has recently gone through a makeover. The green and white awning, polished-brass railings and etched-glass front door speak of a simpler, more genteel period.

Liz hops out and says, "Five minutes, ten tops. Do we have any dinner plans for tonight? I want the correct wardrobe."

"I'm pretty sure that we are going to have to meet

the gang later today, so business casual will work. Maybe something for later."

"You mean you don't like me in your rugby shirt?"

I am sure that I am blushing. "That's not what I meant. Like jeans and a sweater if we go out."

"I think I'll over pack. Between the boys and Billy, I'm not sure we are in control of our social life just yet."

"Sadly, I think you are right. Liz, get a move on it. I'd like to be on the road when Billy calls in twenty minutes."

"Yes sir." She gives a mock salute and runs up the stairs, two at a time.

I remember playing hockey at the MDC rink across the street. I was a terrible hockey player. For a guy who was a good athlete, whenever I strapped something to my feet — skates or skis — all hope was lost. Balance gone — coordination gone — and it is hard to pick up a girl lying on your back in snow or ice — and besides, hockey games were always around 4 in the morning, or so it seemed.

Further up the street is one of the first large-screen, basically stand-alone, movie theaters. Although it has probably been subdivided into eight theaters by now, it used to have only two. So much for progress. I recently heard that the bean counters spend more time worrying about the cost of popcorn oil and the containers into which that unforgettable greasy white stuff was placed (bags versus cups) than about the quality of the movie that was playing.

I am not sure which startled me more, the vibration of the cell phone or Liz opening the door. I raise a finger to indicate wait a minute.

"Callahan." I listen to the voice at the other end of the line.

"I'll tell Detective Browne." I push the red button and for emphasis I snapped it shut. That's why I liked the older cell phones — much more expressive.

"Tell Detective Browne what?" Liz gets in the car and swings a very expensive-looking leather overnight bag into the back seat.

"That the team is meeting at the Captain's house at four. We are expected."

"Who called?"

"Spinelli, who if we believe Billy, is on the right side of the equation, even though he does seem to bend the rules a little."

"Bending is one thing, breaking is another. All the pieces do not yet fit together. If this was a jigsaw puzzle, I'd say the edges are not even in place."

"True, but you are assuming a traditional four-sided puzzle. I had a friend who made high-end jigsaw puzzles out of wood and he did one that was elliptical. It was great because you were forced out of the box, so to speak, to put the pieces together."

"I am extremely uncomfortable with the CIA's participation in this. I don't blame Billy, he doesn't make policy."

"And do you think Spinelli makes policy?" Although we were colleagues, I am not ready to accept Billy's assessment.

"I really want to hear what Billy has to say. I must admit what he has already told us makes sense intuitively. I am still struggling with the fact that I didn't have a clue of what was happening in the area of law enforcement about which I am supposed to know a lot."

"What we really don't understand is the specifics of Billy's involvement. He says he didn't kill anyone, but who did and why didn't Billy reach out to someone?"

"Maintaining his cover may have been more important."

"Ah, but why?" I am trying to develop a theory. "It has

got to be more than the FBI and CIA's lack of cooperation with one another. If I was a gambling man —"

"You wouldn't have met with your Captain in the first place. The odds weren't good at all."

"So true, Ms. State Police Detective, but then I wouldn't have met you."

"Touché!" Liz pokes me in the side — rapier like.

"But to the point..." Liz rolls her eyes to signal she heard, but ignored my wit. "We need to know the story behind Billy's story. For example, who killed those goons, why did he take the fall and who else is involved?"

"That pretty much sums it up. Although we have made contact with Billy, we still know jack shit." Liz voice reeks with sarcasm.

I reach for my vibrating cell phone. "Callahan." I listen carefully. "You sure?" I ask the voice. "Your call. See you in about an hour."

"Billy?"

"He wants us to meet him face-to-face."

"Where?"

"Ipswich!"

"How could he set something up way out there in such a short time?"

"Liz, all I know is that he wants us to go up to Castle Hill, park in the Crane's Beach lot and take a walk along the beach. If we are not being followed, Billy will join us."

"Actually, I hate to admit it, his plan makes sense. We'll have the entire trip to watch for a tail. Unless Billy is setting us up, no one would ever dream of a meeting on the North Shore. He's quite innovative, isn't he?"

"Well, yes."

"Chris, are you listening to me?"

"Very much so. You said unless Billy is setting us up. Are

you getting any vibes that we are being set up?"

"There is no question we are being used. However, I think Billy needs to share his story with us because he knows he is a marked man and if they get to him...bang! Sorry to sound dramatic, but let's face it, if half of what we've already heard today is true, there is a lot going on about which we are in the dark. I also think that by telling us, Billy may be buying some insurance."

"Term or whole life? I'm not trying to be cute. The more we know, the more at risk we are. Correct?"

"Yes, but it spreads out the odds. And cop killing, even ex-cop killing is still frowned upon." Liz tries to make our lives...or rather deaths, sound important. If this is as complicated as I think, we are very, very minor players, who will be missed by all those concerned for about ten minutes.

"If it makes you feel any better, I brought some insurance of my own. See the duffle in the bag seat? The canvas one; L.L. Bean — not Gucci. Open it."

Liz leans over the front seat. It takes every bit of will power I can muster not to give her derriere a quick pat.

"Point well taken, Mr. Callahan." She reaches into the bag and removes our body armor and a rather ugly-looking sawed-off shotgun — 12-gauge, pump-action Remington. Without so much as a second's hesitation, Liz pulls her sweatshirt over her head, under which she has only a tee shirt, dons the bulletproof vest and slips her sweatshirt back on. She then pumps a shell into the chamber.

"Is that where the phrase riding shotgun comes from?"

"If you want to compare your classic Chevy to a stage coach...yes. Put on your vest and let's go."

"Yes, boss."

"Glad we got that straightened out." Liz gives me a

quick kiss...and pats my thigh. Quite an improvement. I was expecting a punch.

CHAPTER THIRTY-SIX

The ride up to Ipswich is uneventful. So is the route we take. There are basically three choices: Route 95, new and wide but too far west; Route 1, old and narrow but still too far west; and Route 128, newer than Route 1 and wider but too far east. Consequently, to get to Ipswich, you will spend a significant portion of the journey on small, winding roads. Not good for a summer weekend but perfect for spotting a tail…and shaking it if necessary.

Ipswich is one of the oldest towns in Massachusetts, founded in 1633. Although originally a fishing center, tourism has become the dominant economic driver. The population increases in direct proportion to the temperature. I personally like the so-called shoulders of the season, when the air is warm, the restaurants are still open, but the visiting hoards have returned to their lairs.

Castle Hill was the summer estate of the Crane family — the other toilet company. The buildings and gardens have been well maintained over the years, largely as a result of a booming wedding business. The beach, Crane's Beach, is one of the most beautiful stretches of sand — anywhere. We arrive pretty much on time and park in the empty parking lot.

"Do we pack the big stuff?" Liz pats the shotgun.

"Be careful! You've got a shell in the chamber."

"No need to panic, I have the safety on." Liz has the uncanny ability to make me both concerned and relieved at the same time.

"I think a bulge in my sweat suit that big will draw attention to us."

Liz starts to laugh hysterically.

I get it.

"Chris," Liz is trying to regain her composure, "maybe we should leave the shotgun under the seat." She starts to laugh again, this time with a bit more tension than before.

"Let's go! I don't want to keep Billy waiting."

"I think you are a big party pooper." She leans over and gives me a quick peck on the cheek.

"You just want to make fun of me."

"You make it so easy." At least I got another kiss.

After locking the car, we start down the path toward the beach below. Liz grabs my hand...firmly.

I give her hand a squeeze back, turn and look into her eyes. "It'll be fine," I whisper, not entirely convinced.

"We should look at the bright side," Liz rallies. "At least it's a beautiful early spring day; the sun is shining; the sky is blue and we are together, blissfully walking toward a gorgeous beach. Provided of course, there's no quicksand, everything is great — as good as it gets." Liz's voice falters. "Who cares about double murders, terrorism, the Mob, the crazies, the drug cartels? It's a simply gorgeous day." My companion is clearly about to lose it.

"Detective Browne, pull it together...now!" I hope I don't sound too heavy, but this is not the time to fall apart.

She takes a deep breath. "Right. Sorry. It's all a bit

weird. I feel very disconnected. Everything Billy said was new to me. It shouldn't have been a surprise, but it was. Obviously I wasn't doing my job very well."

It is obvious what is bothering Liz. "Look, there is no way you can compare the combined resources of the CIA and the FBI with those of the Massachusetts State Police. Please try to remember that the ball started rolling overseas; Mexico, the Far East, the Middle East, not Chelsea or East Boston. Without that connection, the picture was never apparent. If it makes you feel better, lest you forget, I was the one who built the case to put Billy in jail for life. And he was my best friend."

"Thanks. You are right. Let's get to the bottom of this and if there is a snake, let's cut off its head." Liz has gone from passive to super-aggressive in less time than it takes to say — Callahan you are a stupid mother for getting involved in someone else's mess.

"Welcome to Castle Hill."

"Billy, you scared the shit out of me."

"Me, too."

"Sorry about that, chief. I guess I still retain a bit of prison humor. It's been what…three days. I would invite you to join me in a picnic, but I didn't have time to properly provision for an outing, although I did bring a Dunkin' Donuts coffee for the lovely Detective Browne...Liz and an unsweetened iced tea for you, Skippy." If anything, Billy looks younger than he did last time I saw him.

"Shall we walk, talk and sip or find a place to sit?" Liz is back in stride.

"I suggest we bear right up there," Billy points to a fork in the path. "It leads to an opening with a couple of benches. It's only accessible from the path, unless you are a mountain goat, so I think we are reasonably safe. Also you will note that the parking lot is far from filled, like not at all."

I am amazed how well Billy has planned for everything. He has only had a couple of hours to plan our meeting, but I guess if you work for the Agency you develop certain skill sets.

"As I recall," Billy starts, "we left off with your question, Liz, about my involvement and that of others. After the meeting between the Dons and the drug lords, there were a number of murders in many east coast Chinatowns. Most everyone attributed it to fighting between gangs for turf, but it was orchestrated by the Mexicans. Since the Oriental gangs are secret, local law enforcement officials didn't realize that those who were being killed, to the extent that they even knew the extent of the murders, were the gang leaders not mere members. The word within the Family was that it was time to reassert control. And they did. Very subtly. Some of the remaining Asian gang members were even recruited so that the face of the organization remained the same to both the outside and to a certain portion of society who were being provided protection."

Billy sips his coffee. "It's still hot."

"Then what?" I ask.

"Then came another meeting. A very important meeting."

"Liz, were you aware of violence in the Asian community?" I am not sure how much the Asian gangs are linked with traditional organized crime.

"There is a lot about the Asian gangs that we don't know. Billy is right. It is a very closed society and I am sure there are homicides that go unreported every day. Unlike the conventional Mob hit, where the body is left as a calling card, the Asians leave nothing. Since many of these folks are undocumented, there is no trace that they even existed, let alone died. Also, the gang involvement was thought to be limited to their communities."

"Not so. That was the problem. There wasn't enough in the Asian community to keep all the soldiers satisfied. They started to step on the Families' toes in non-Asian areas." Billy is very well informed, which leads me to conclude that his role might have been understated.

"About the meeting?" Liz wants to get back on track.

"Again I am asked to drive and again I am able to plant bugs. This meeting is part two of the plan; crazies against Latinos, except the crazies are a lot more respectable and powerful than I ever imagined."

Suddenly there is a rustling of branches.

CHAPTER THIRTY-SEVEN

Both Liz and I reach for our weapons and aim toward the source of the noise. I thought Billy had checked this place out. It's a little too early in the season for a couple of kids fooling around in the woods. I glance over at Billy. He remains unmoved. Led by a very fat male raccoon, five little kits waddle through the brush, followed by mom. They completely ignore us and continue down the path toward the parking lot.

"If I weren't a lady, I'd have peed in my pants." Liz drops her Browning into the canvas tote bag.

"It is remotely possible that we are a bit, how does one say it, stressed out." I return my weapon to its holster.

"No shit, Sherlock." Billy always has something witty to say.

"Shall we go back to the meeting?" Liz regains her composure.

"It was like a scene out of The Godfather. Since the location was a secret, I would get directions from one of the gumbos in the back seat as I was driving like, take a right at the third stoplight or take a left at A-1 Pizza. It took close to two hours to get to a place that was only fifteen minutes away."

"How did you know it was only fifteen minutes away?" I thought that it was a logical question.

"Because I recognized the place, Skippy. It was in Hyde Park, right around the corner from where we played baseball."

"The old warehouse?" I asked. "Wasn't it all boarded up? I remember being told to stay away from the place. I always thought it would burn down or blow down some night."

"A brilliant piece of camouflage. Once inside, it was high-tech all the way; security screening; teleconferencing on huge screens; computer hookups; the works. I told you that the business school types were involved."

"Did you get inside?"

"Not exactly."

"What do you mean…not exactly? You've just told us what the place looked like."

"Patience, my friend, patience, unless you guys are in a hurry to go somewhere."

"Actually, we've got to be at Captain Hancock's at four to meet with everyone involved because of your unexpected death," Liz explains.

"Billy, it was unexpected, wasn't it?" I ask.

"Let me finish my story and then you decide. I was somewhat surprised that my little bugs weren't discovered, although they had been pretty well field-tested by the boys at Langley. It's simply marvelous to have a budget that large to make cool little things. By the way, the bugs had video as well as audio capabilities."

"Are we going to be able to make the meeting with the Captain?"

"Detective Browne, I wouldn't let you miss the meeting for all the tea in China." Billy smiles.

"Let me continue. When we arrived, only the big wigs went inside. The drivers stayed with the cars. Nobody could leave or use a cell phone. We just hung around and talked. I just listened. Got to know who was attending the meeting by listening to drivers brag about the people they brought and how they were more important than the other drivers' passengers. It helped us later on to identify some of the voices."

"Who was there? We need names." Liz speaks altogether too fast.

"My concern is not the Mob. They are local and are merely a small piece in the game, but I won't drop names. However, the other folks in attendance, including those who electronically joined the meeting, were my concern. If you ever doubted that some of our so-called leaders are more than willing to sell the fundamental principles of America for a handful of silver or a cupful of oil, dispel the thought. The purpose of the meeting was to cut a deal between the Dons and the crazies to deport, one way or another, all Hispanics and other illegals, especially Asians. Until this meeting, it was generally thought that these extremists were just a fringe operation at best, under-funded, under-connected and few in number. Wrong. Not only were they receiving money with which to buy weapons from the Middle East, they were being sold weapons from United States stockpiles. That's right folks, they didn't have to go to arms merchants in former Soviet republics, they were able to get guns here. The money laundering was considered a joke being played on the towel heads. The crazies took their money, but knew exactly what they were doing and they were operating with impunity because they were being given protection. The Dons didn't care about illegal aliens and our immigration policies, they wanted to regain control of the drug trade."

"Billy, this is too much to absorb and sounds like a soap opera. Let me get this straight. Money from the Middle East is almost irrelevant. The Mob is almost irrelevant. The Mexicans are almost irrelevant. It's the radical fringe about whom we should be paying attention...correct?"

"Skippy, if it was a fringe, it would be the price of democracy, but it is a lot larger than a fringe, with roots going right up to the seats of power in Washington."

"Don't take this the wrong way Billy, but you are talking conspiracy on a grand scale."

"Detective Browne, grand is an understatement. The adage in almost any crime investigation is follow the money. The Agency followed the money. I followed the money. We made a mistake by assuming that giving the money to the crazies was simply a disruptive play from the terrorist playbook. However, the recipients of the money had another playbook. The Agency, together with almost every other law enforcement branch in America and Mexico is closely monitoring the drug wars. It is out of control. People are being gunned down in streets both here and across the border. Millions — no billions of dollars are at stake. Remember that the FBI was supposed to be watching the radical fringe, but the Bureau always seemed slow to do anything, if they did anything at all."

"Which explains the Agency's extra-jurisdictional activities?" Liz is still angry about the State Police, and presumably the BPD, being cut out of things.

"Liz, I am not going to give you or anyone else a lecture about National Security or any of that bullshit, but what if I told you that one of the voices positively identified speaking at the meeting belonged to the second assistant director of the Federal Bureau of Investigation?"

"Jesus, Joseph and Mary!!" My mother, bless her soul,

would have washed out my mouth with soap.

"Not to be outdone, also in attendance and actively participating in the meeting was a Congressman, two former Congressmen, a sitting Governor and a former Governor, together with a number of very well-connected CEOs of business and industry."

"And why hasn't any of this become public?" Liz sounds skeptical. I am feeling a bit uncomfortable with all of this, as well.

"Blame him!" Billy points a finger at me.

"Wait a minute, what did I do?"

"Your job!" Billy starts to smile. "I am only kidding, Skippy. Well, not really. Before I had a chance to listen to the audio from the meeting and edit the rough video and make copies, Spinelli asked me to follow a couple of guys who were suspected of selling components which could be used as detonator timers. Although technically a domestic surveillance, there was a thread that connected these guys with al-Qaeda-trained operatives who might be working here."

"Let me ask a question." Liz was not asking for permission. "Was the CIA going it alone because there was a connection to an ongoing international investigation or because they didn't trust working with the FBI?"

"A little of both. Well, a lot of both. The Agency was acutely aware of the shit storm that domestic spying would cause, so everything had a connection, albeit a bit circuitous at times, to international intelligence. Like this time. These guys were selling the stuff to the crazies to use to blow up mosques, car bomb drug shipments...whatever. Coincidently, the components were the same as were used to detonate explosive devices in Spain and several bombs that never exploded, both here and abroad."

"I guess I am not surprised that the CIA operates in such a high-handed manner. They have never been team players." Liz is clearly miffed.

"Detective...Liz, it's not totally high handed and we have been team players more than you know. It's hard to get a warm and fuzzy feeling when you don't know who to trust."

"It's not about warm and fuzzy. It's about something more important." Liz is virtually screaming.

"Sorry to say it, but it really is about National Security. Not the kind leaders hide behind when tough questions are being asked, but the kind that saves lives. I know that a lot of things are excused under the aegis of National Security, but there is a lot going on about which you don't know... can't know."

"Billy, this is beginning to sound like the exchange between Jack Nicholson and Tom Cruise in A Few Good Men. We can handle the truth. We may not like it, but we can handle it. Let's get back on track."

"You're right. Sorry. Liz, you and Skippy have each put yourself on the line...now and many times before. Please understand that I have also put myself out there. I am not asking for accolades, just understanding that I am doing what I think is best, based on the information I have, which may not be the same as you have. Think about it, when you guys volunteered for this assignment, I was no more than an escaped double murderer, but your sense of fair play required you to participate. Sometimes fair play gets a lot of people killed. No more digressions."

Billy opens a bottle of water and takes a long and well-deserved drink.

"I followed the two suspects to a three-decker in Dorchester. They cautiously entered the building, like they weren't sure it was the right place. I didn't have any listening devices, so I watched them. I saw them enter the second floor unit. The hall light silhouetted them at the door. Suddenly, I heard gun shots and I watched both men drop. A minute later, two other men, obviously professionals, left the building. They walked to the corner. A black Lincoln Town Car stopped. They got in and drove away. No screeching tires — nothing to draw attention to themselves. I debated whether to go upstairs and see what I could find out and then report, or simply leave and tell Spinelli what I saw. I opted, rather foolishly for the former. Within less than thirty seconds from when I entered the room, three plainclothes cops from your precinct showed up, guns drawn. Clearly I was set up, but by whom? And the rest is history."

"Why didn't you say anything?" I almost plead.

"Skippy, at that point I didn't know who to trust. I had a recording that could shake the very foundation of the American political structure. I had the reputation for being a Mob loyalist and my only potential savior was Pete Spinelli, who was a bit out of venue. So I decided to be cool and hope everything would work itself out. I wasn't worried about prison. I was connected, and I was a crazy cold-blooded murderer."

Billy raises the water bottle again. "Wish it was a Guinness."

I am always amazed at how Billy keeps his cool.

"What happened in jail?" Liz's tone has softened.

"At first, I used the time to put the pieces together, then to figure out how to get to the outside without being killed. This may sound a bit over the top, but Spinelli and I had discussed the possibility that I might end up in the can at some point in time and we had a plan. It took a few months longer than I would have wished but…Here's Billy!"

"With half the law enforcement community after you." I am not sure whether Liz's comment was a warning or an expression of sympathy.

"Actually, it's probably closer to three-quarters. I am more concerned about the Feds than anyone else. They are the wild card."

"Billy, what about the recording?" I can buy almost everything he has said so far, but a recording of the meeting would shed quite a different light — like credibility.

"I was hoping you'd ask. I did not spend the last forty-eight hours hanging out at IHOP." Billy reaches into his jacket and produces a CD. "Do you have a CD player in your antique? I suggest you listen on your way to your four o'clock meeting, for which you really should change."

I reach for the disk.

"I made four copies. Sent one to a safe post office box I've been using to deliver things to Spinelli, but he probably hasn't checked it recently. Remind him to do so. I sent a copy to the only other person I trust other than you and Pete, Father Burke. And I have a copy right here." He pats his jacket.

I never thought Billy O'Brien to be a religious person, but then again, I guess I really don't know as much about him as I thought.

"Where are you going to be? How can I reach you?"

"I will find you, never fear. I have my ways."

"Billy, don't fuck around. I…we went through a shit load to find you!" I scream.

"Actually, I found you. However, Skippy, take this cell phone. It's clean and has one number stored in it…mine. I think we should talk before you meet with Feinstein."

"Feinstein? Why him?" I sense that I have lost rather

than gained another puzzle piece.

"Listen to the CD. We'll talk again later. Hurry along, you two. Wouldn't be good form to show up late. Think of the gossip it would cause." Billy laughs, turns and walks down the path. "And Skippy, don't forget to shave."

CHAPTER THIRTY-EIGHT

I don't think that either Liz or I care whether we are being followed or not. And at the speed we were traveling, even a twelve-year-old on a bike could keep up with us. We are riveted. The quality of the recording is perfect. I'm not able to recognize the speakers from their voices initially. I wish we had had time to listen with Billy providing commentary. Without warning, we hear a voice.

"It's not?" We both stammered at the same time.

I just barely avoid rear-ending the car in front of me.

"Pull over," Liz commands.

"Good idea. I want to hear that again."

I spot a closed for the season ice cream stand. I am sweating and I don't think it is because of the car's heater. I replay the last portion of the CD.

"No fuckin' doubt about it." I guess I am not shocked at Liz's reaction. I have to admit that the order of all things has been turned upside down.

"I can't disagree about the voice, but I think we should listen to the entire meeting before we jump to conclusions."

"I don't mean to be harsh, but anyone whose voice is on this recording is not a good guy."

"There is a possibility that — "

"Chris, just get real. I'm as shocked as you are, but what we heard is what we heard."

"Liz, on the face of it, attendance at the meeting puts someone in a bad light, but in order to put everything in context, and not prejudge, we have to listen to the entire meeting."

"It's going to take a lot to convince me to change my mind, based on what Billy told us and what I just heard."

"If you had simply listened to the CD without Billy's comments, would you feel differently?"

"Possibly, but — " Liz is backing down...a little.

"See what we are doing? We have accepted everything Billy said as gospel."

"But the recording?"

"How do we know it's even authentic? Billy could have cut and pasted the whole thing."

"To what end?"

"I'm not sure, but nothing has made sense since we first started. There are so many loose ends." Maybe I don't want to know the truth. Maybe I can't handle it.

"Billy's explanation is the only way everything fits together." Liz is also grasping for straws.

"Correction, it's the only explanation we've heard."

"I agree. I need a few minutes to digest this. Chris, is there some place where I can get a coffee and go to the ladies' room?"

"I can't vouch for its cleanliness, but there is a gas station at the intersection with Route 1. I think they have a Ma's Donuts there, also."

"Should we call Billy and see what he says?"

"Liz, I think we should..." I raise one finger, "...get to the gas station and get something to drink." I could use a beer right about now. "Then I think we should listen to the balance of the recording. Whether it's real or a fake, we need to know what's on it."

"Chris, I think we should assume the CD is authentic and unedited."

"Why?"

"In many ways, Billy's story is the only way everything fits together."

"You're probably right."

"What time is it?"

"We're okay. It's only two, but we've got to get moving." I get back out onto Route 133.

Part of me doesn't want to hear any more. Part of me wants to come up with another explanation. Part of me wants the other parts to shut up and listen.

For the next half hour, we hear things I thought only possible on TV. I am really scared now, not for me alone, but for most people who believe that the fringe is just that: a few people at the far end of either side of issues. I never imagined that the passion of hatred ran so deep in this country. Without being aware of anything except the CD, I pull into my garage and turn off the car. "But it's not done." Liz's voice is filled with desperation.

"We can listen in my apartment. The sound will be even better."

"It's not the sound that concerns me, it's the content. Let's hurry."

I reach under the seat and grab the shotgun, eject the shell, lean over the front seat to get my duffle and drop it in the bag. Liz is already out of the car. She opens the back door, retrieves her clothes and starts to jog toward my house.

"Wait!" She stops. "Take a deep breath. The coast is far from clear and lest we forget, we are still not sure we know who the bad guys are and who the good guys are."

"Chris, I think I've got a pretty good idea, but being cautious makes a lot of sense.

Once inside the apartment, Liz says, "Don't start the CD without me. I want to freshen up and change so we can leave as late as possible." She closes the bedroom door.

I could definitely use a drink and a nap and a valium. I place the CD into the player and cue it to where we were listening. The temptation to push Play is really big, but Liz would kill me and I'm not convinced figuratively.

I decide a cup of hot tea might settle my nerves. Actually, my nerves are just fine, I'm just pissed off. I need to focus that anger. I can't blame myself for putting Billy in jail, although I wish he had trusted me a little more back then. He seems sanguine about the experience, so I should be as well. I am struggling to find the right word. I put the kettle on the stove and knock on the bedroom door.

"I really need a quick shower and shave. Are you almost done?"

"I'm through with the bathroom, I'm just getting dressed. Come in!"

Did I just hear the voice of a gorgeous woman telling me to come into a bedroom, albeit mine, while she is getting dressed? I open the door, peek and then enter. I guess after seeing Liz in my rugby shirt everything is anticlimactic, although she looks great in a black bra and panties.

"Hurry up, you pervert."

I quickly strip down to my boxers and retreat into the bathroom, turn on the water as hot as it gets and step in. I'm one of those kinds of guys who likes to shave while showering. If I nick myself, the blood rinses away. Three minutes is all I need to feel relatively rejuvenated.

Assuming Liz is done, I re-enter my bedroom with

only a towel wrapped around my beet-red body.

"My, don't you look good enough to eat." Liz walks over and gives my towel a fake tug. "Maybe, later. Hurry up. It's almost time to go."

I set the Guinness Book of World Records getting dressed.

"Ready?" I ask.

"Here's your tea. You forgot and left the water boiling." My mom used to say the same thing.

The CD only lasts another ten minutes. The finale is everyone saying good-bye like it was a high school reunion. I have a sudden urge to throw up, but I insert a blank CD into the player instead.

"Insurance," I say holding up the duplicate disc.

"I hope we don't need it and I'm still not sure from whom."

I walk across the room, slide a Matisse etching, an original, slightly to the left, revealing a slot.

"What is that?" Liz asks.

"A slot," I adroitly reply.

"I hate a smart ass. I know it's a slot. Where does it go?"

"Ahh so, Charlie Chan, goes to strong safe in basement where no one would think to look." I don't think my accent fools anyone.

"You are far more clever than you appear at first glance."

"Detective Browne, you need to improve your skills of observation. Let's go and call Billy from the road."

"Chris?" Liz sounds almost child-like. "What do you intend to do with the disc?"

"Depends."

"On what?"

"On whether I hear what I want from our assembled

colleagues."

"Which is unlikely, right?"

"Highly."

"Then what?"

"I'll probably shoot someone." I pat my ankle.

"Mr. Callahan, what I am about to say is very important. Listen! I care a lot about you and I have an idea of how you operate and what motivates you. I feel the same way about what we've heard, but the difference is that I am still a member of the law enforcement community and I want to do this right. If I can avoid shooting someone, I will. I want this sordid mess to be cleaned up, but it's got to be the right way. Remember that cutting off the head of the snake is important, provided we have the head, not the rattle."

"Very well said. I'll just shoot him in the ass."

I guess I deserve the punch Liz delivers with entirely more force than necessary. Nervous energy.

CHAPTER THIRTY-NINE

I elect to take the scenic route to our meeting: from Harvard Square out Cambridge Street through Inman Square to Lechmere Square (also the name of a store chain that no longer exists) and cross into Boston. I figure the additional mileage will give me enough time to get Billy's take on what we have heard. I dial his number from the cell phone he gave me. No answer.

"Shit!"

"What's wrong?"

"Billy doesn't answer his phone."

"Chris, try again. Maybe you dialed the wrong number." Liz tries to sound reassuring but she forgot that Billy had programmed the number into the phone he gave me. I push redial, but still, no answer. I feel a wave of nausea, or is it panic?

"Other than waving around the disc, do you have a plan?" Liz doesn't sound very confident either.

"I want to ask Billy how he thinks we should handle the meeting. Maybe we simply ask the Captain to use his CD player and see what happens?"

"That might not be as bad of an idea as you seem to be implying. No one else has heard the recording, so we'll be able to watch how each reacts to the CD."

"It's really only the reaction of one person about whom I most worry."

"Chris, are you so sure about what we listened to? I think that the way in which each of the group responds will be very, very enlightening. And what's the choice?"

Before I answer, the phone rings. Instinctively I answer my cell.

"Callahan." I try to sound a lot more self-assured than I feel. The problem is that the phone is still ringing. It's Billy's phone. "Billy?"

"Sorry, Skippy, but nature was calling. I'm not used to drinking that much coffee. At least it was decaf, otherwise I'd be off the wall. Only kidding. What's up?"

I don't fathom how Billy can appear to be so calm.

"We've got to be at Captain Hancock's in ten minutes. How should I play this?"

"How should we play this?" Liz snatches the phone from me.

"I love domestic disputes. Put us on speaker, Liz... please." Liz gives me a dirty look.

"Here are my thoughts," Billy pauses just long enough for both Liz and me to move closer to the phone. "The front door of the Captain's house is never locked during the day, but when it is opened a beeping sound goes off in the pantry to alert James. Almost everyone rings the doorbell and waits to be admitted."

I forgot that Billy had worked for Captain Hancock before Pete Spinelli, so it made sense that he knew the ins and outs of the brownstone.

"I am not following you." I have no idea where Billy is going.

"I will walk into the Captain's house exactly fifteen

minutes after you and Liz enter. In order for this to work, you need to get James into the library. Ask for something to drink. I am sure you can come up with something believable."

"Billy, I'm not sure it's such a good idea that you show up." Liz is clearly concerned. For Billy or for us or for both.

"I'm always the life of the party. Liz, please explain."

"You are considered an escaped murderer — armed and presumed dangerous."

"Oh that...the least of my concerns. You guys got dragged into this mess because the best minds in law enforcement collectively figured that Skippy was the only one who could bring me out into the open. While they were right, once I was able to listen to the CD and get it copied, the stakes increased and the odds changed."

"In whose favor?" I ask.

"Short term, since I'm dead, the odds are in my favor. Long term, the CD is so explosive, I'm not sure. It's my turn to ask you something, Skippy."

"Shoot." Bad choice of words.

"Do you intend to play the CD at the meeting?"

"Probably."

"That's what I thought and I'll bet you made a copy and put it in a safe place. Liz, do you agree that it's a good idea to play the CD?"

"I don't think we have an option. We need to stop these people here and now."

"My dear detective, please do not assume that we three are going to be able to stop what's happening out there. All we can do is delay, disrupt and temporarily destroy. These people are very much like any other extremist group, they will never give up, they will die first and even if we kill them all, others will rise to take their place."

"You make this seem like Armageddon."

"It is."

"Billy, we've got to park and go in."

"Fifteen minutes from the time you enter."

"Are we all winging this?" Liz would be happier with a plan.

"Improvise." Billy and I answer together. Liz pushes the red button and tosses the phone on the seat between us.

Some days if I didn't have bad luck, I'd have no luck at all. Needless to say, there weren't any parking spaces on Joy Street or any place else on Beacon Hill, but I did find a two-hour meter on Beacon Street, a couple of blocks away.

"Liz, do you have any quarters?" I ask.

She opens her pocketbook. "I've got two."

"So do I. One hour. Do you think we'll be done?"

"One way or another."

"Now that's encouraging."

Billy's phone starts to vibrate. It's a text. Better get a move on it, everyone is already there. XXOO. We both smile at Billy's sense of humor.

"Has he always been like that?" Liz asks.

"You mean funny or crazy?"

"At this point, the line between the two is fine indeed."

CHAPTER FORTY

We walk as quickly as we can, aware of the precision required to get Billy into the house. I have a second sense that we are being watched...by Billy I hope. I haven't discarded the fact that Billy is still very much a target, despite his rather aloof attitude.

"Do you think that Billy is watching us?" Liz asks. It is unnerving that she and I seem to be on the same wavelength.

"I hope so. I think the clock starts fifteen minutes after we enter, not fifteen minutes from when we parked."

"That's a relief. Let's slow down. I don't want to be out of breath when we arrive. It's not lady-like." Liz reaches out, grabs my hand and gives it a squeeze. "There's always tomorrow."

"Let's hope so." I squeeze back.

I swing the iron gate open. "Please, after you, my dear."

"Chivalry is not dead."

"It is alive and well in Cambridge, Massachusetts." Whether our banter is a stall or an attempt to relax is totally irrelevant, because the large front door swings open.

"Everyone is waiting for you in the library." The ubiquitous James greets us.

"Thank you." I try to sound like this is just another social visit with my former employer.

Liz and I follow James down the hall. I take a quick peek over my shoulder at the front door. I hope Billy is right.

"Detective Browne and Lieutenant Callahan." James announces and then exits. What's with the rank?

The assembled look no worse for wear. In fact, it almost appears as if a load has been lifted from their collective shoulders — Billy.

"Chris...Detective Browne...welcome. It has been a rather exhausting 24 hours, hasn't it? Please be seated." Captain Hancock sounds a little too formal.

I feel like asking for whom has it been exhausting?

"I am sorry that we weren't able to talk to Billy or bring him to you so that you could speak with him. I guess a lot of answers died with Billy." I try to sound indifferent. Liz looks equally disappointed. I am not sure how long either of us can maintain this façade.

"I know you've both been through a lot. No one wanted to talk to Billy more than I did." Pete Spinelli sounds sincere, but I lack Billy's confidence in any of the assembled, except Liz.

"I have just one question," Liz rises from the leather wing chair. I think the façade is about to crumble.

Liz waits a mini-second before continuing. "Why was it the Mob was able to find Billy and all of your collective Departments couldn't?"

"It's not as simple as that," Roger Feinstein starts.

I am beginning to really hate this guy, as opposed to just plain hating him.

"Billy chose who was going to find him and it wasn't us."

"Why would he choose someone who was going to kill him?" I ask.

"Did he think he was safer with the Mob than with you?" Liz adds.

"He probably didn't think it through." I wonder if everyone in the U.S. Attorney's office is as smug as Feinstein.

"With all his close connections with law enforcement, I would think that he would have sought out at least one of you." Liz tries to make eye contact with each attendee. Pete Spinelli blinks once too often.

I glance down at my watch. "Captain, could you ask James to bring me some water? My throat is a little scratchy."

"I'm sorry. I haven't asked anyone if they'd like refreshments." Predictably, Captain Hancock pushes the button under his desk to summon James.

"Sir?" The butler asks upon entering.

"James, would you please bring refreshments?"

"Certainly, sir." I wonder if our attendance at four o'clock was simply the epilogue of a meeting that began earlier in the afternoon. There is an undercurrent of tension. Is it because of Billy's death or something else... like his non-death? I don't have the impression everyone is on the same page.

The atmosphere is certainly not conducive to an Irish wake. The Captain asks for sparkling water...not champagne. Even Commander Marshall orders a Coke. I glance at my watch. Billy has had almost seven minutes to get into the house.

No one says a thing. Very creepy.

"Well, I guess my part in this matter is over." I hope someone responds. "I want you to know that unless anyone has a strenuous objection, I plan on attending Billy's funeral." No comments.

I glance over in Liz's direction. Almost imperceptibly, she shrugs her shoulders. I rise.

"The Bureau would like to thank you for your offer to help. It is too bad we weren't able to get O'Brien on the carpet."

I resist responding to Feinstein's arrogance.

"Chris, you have the Department's thanks as well. Maybe we could have a relaxing dinner...soon. You, too, Detective Browne." Captain Hancock seems a bit more animated. Maybe, the thought of a fine dinner is settling.

"You seem to have some police talk to finish and since I appear to be a fifth wheel, I'll take my leave." No one objects.

Turning toward Liz, I whisper, "Call you later." She nods.

Just as I turn to go, James opens the living room door with the drinks and a platter of sandwiches. Structure is everything in the Hancock household, which stills holds to the tradition of crust-less cucumber sandwiches at teatime.

"Thank you, James," I say as he proffers a glass.

"I assumed you wanted still water, sir."

"Yes."

"I want to personally thank you for sticking your necks out, and Chris...good work." Pete Spinelli extends his hand, which I take. It is the first warmth I've felt since entering.

I sip my water, as much to think through the next phase of our little drama, as to quench my growing thirst.

"Oh, by the way, there is something that I'd like you all to hear before I leave. I know you'll find it very enlightening." I hold up the CD. "Detective Browne and I did."

"Callahan," Feinstein says, "is this the appropriate time to listen to a CD?"

"Don't you think that it depends on what is on the disc?" Liz moves next to me.

"Chris, I know that this is not a joke, but an explanation is in order."

"I think not, Captain. I think that listening is what is in order." That certainly got everyone's attention.

"Very well. If you think it's that important. The CD player is over there." The Captain points to a cabinet in the corner. It wouldn't be proper to keep electronics in plain view.

The dynamics of this group is definitely weird, especially considering the positions and experience of those gathered. Captain Hancock is defensive, Commander Marshall is clueless, Roger Feinstein is being an asshole and Pete Spinelli is acting as if he lost his best friend. Maybe no one really knows that Billy is alive and well and, hopefully, waiting outside the library door. I install the CD and notice that Liz has positioned herself next to the door. I wonder to myself, where is her Browning?

"Chris, how long is the recording?" Captain Hancock asks impatiently. "And what is it about?"

"It depends on whether you want to listen to the whole thing, which is about forty minutes or simply a portion I have identified as providing the most revelations — that's only about ten minutes. Please listen carefully. This really requires your 100% attention. To answer your second question, the CD records a secret meeting that took place a little over a year ago."

"May I ask where did you get this?" Pete starts to pace yet again.

"A friend," I answer. I am not sure when and how Billy

is going to make his entrance.

"I don't want to be rude — " Attorney Feinstein begins.

"Then don't be." Billy walks into the room with a huge smile on his face. "Yes it is me...in the flesh and I want to keep it that way, so gentlemen, may I have your weapons?" To ensure that everyone is paying attention, Billy points a mean-looking 9mm Beretta semi-automatic at the assembled.

The silence is deafening. Billy moves from Commander Marshall, to Captain Hancock, to Feinstein and then to Spinelli, collecting assorted guns.

"But...you're dead." I can't tell if Spinelli is relieved or disappointed.

"Not yet, Pete, and I hope you kept my medal. You know how much that means to me."

"That's how I was sure it was you."

"Well, it wasn't and I didn't kill anyone. The body was a John Doe who had been delivered to the morgue only an hour earlier. I had to make it look real. I needed a little time to complete a few unfinished errands and I wasn't interested in getting bumped off by one or more of your respective henchmen."

"Detective Browne, since you apparently still have a weapon, place Mr. O'Brien under arrest! Now!" Commander Marshall tries to sound authoritative. but his order sounds more like a stammer.

"I respectfully suggest that you all listen to the CD. You asked that we bring Mr. O'Brien to you so that you could speak with him. We have done so. He has gone to great lengths and not insignificant risk to get these recordings, which both Mr. Callahan and I have heard. Please sit down! Commander Marshall, if after listening to the CD and to Mr. O'Brien, you disagree with my decision, you may have my badge."

"That's not all. You are obstructing justice. What about you, Callahan? Why aren't you doing anything?" The former SEAL starts to stand, until Detective Browne removes her Browning from her purse and aims it at him.

"Because Mr. Feinstein, you are not my employer. Second, I have no official standing in the law enforcement community. And third, I think you should listen to the CD."

"Chris, I trust your judgment and I for one have all the time necessary to listen, think and talk." Looking around the room, Captain Hancock continues. "We gave these folks an assignment because we lacked the ability to do it ourselves. They brought Mr. O'Brien to us. He seems more than willing to speak with us and his request that we listen to something is not wholly unreasonable. However, I would like to know what it is we will be hearing."

"May I speak?" Pete Spinelli moves into the middle of the room. "Let me start by saying that Billy O'Brien did not kill those two guys in Dorchester."

"Wait a minute! He was tried and found guilty." That's the most emotion I've ever seen from Commander Marshall.

"True, but only because certain surveillance tapes of the crime scene were not made public."

"What are you talking about, Pete?" The Captain is almost shouting. "Are you saying that the Department overlooked something?"

"No, sir. You were never intended to know about the tapes. And the fact that Chris was the lead officer in the investigation added to the credibility of the conviction. It became apparent that to protect Billy, putting him in prison was the safest thing."

"Who did he have to be protected from?" I wonder if

Feinstein is serving up a smokescreen? It's clear to me that Billy needed protection from a whole lot of folks.

"Lest you forget, Mr. O'Brien's employer of record is organized crime." When you talk to a Harvard lawyer, you should sound like a Harvard lawyer.

"Mr. Feinstein poses another $64,000 question. From whom do I need protection...other than from myself? Let me be so bold as to suggest that each of the four branches of law enforcement represented in this room has a reason to want me dead or at least on ice. To the Boston Police Department, I am a murderer. To the State Police, I am a Mob enforcer. To the CIA, the nature of my employment may be very sensitive and last, but not least, to the FBI, I may have certain information that might be embarrassing or much worse. To respond, Captain Hancock, my innocence is irrefutable." Captain Hancock nods. "Commander Marshall, I think I have convinced Detective Browne that my position with the Families was a cover and that I provided information to several segments of law enforcement, although both the State Police and BPD were pretty much out of the loop."

"Where is this going?" Feinstein is going to have a heart attack if he doesn't stop squirming in his seat.

"I am trying to answer your question. You have gone to great pains to bring me here, so you will have to be patient and listen to what I have to say, which does not include interrupting." Billy has come a long way from Southie. "The CIA's domestic activities in the persona of me, add up to nothing, which is why I'm still alive today."

Pete Spinelli slows his incessant pacing.

"But as to the FBI, now there's a different kettle of fish."

"What do you mean?" Captain Hancock believes that

all cops are good cops, despite decades of seeing bad apples.

"Let's listen to the CD. It was recorded by me. Copies have been made and delivered to appropriate people. Pete, your copy has been sent to our P.O. box. It is important to listen carefully. The audio is surprisingly good, but does require your close attention since sometimes people speak over other people. Voiceprints are being made, but many voices are clearly identifiable."

CHAPTER FORTY-ONE

"Since we are all here, we might as well listen to the whole recording." One of Roger Feinstein's more logical comments.

"Shall I ask James to get some more refreshments?" Captain Hancock is always the perfect host — concerned about his guests, even if they are a bunch of cops. I wonder if good manners are in his DNA?

"It's a little too early for me," I quip. Everyone else nods in concurrence.

Billy walks over to the entertainment center and says, "I would prefer to play the entire recording without interruption, so if you have any questions or comments, just hold them until we're done." He pushes the Play button.

The first couple minutes consist of everyone introducing themselves. "Good afternoon gentlemen, I'm so and so...from...wherever. I am pleased to be in your esteemed company...blah, blah, blah." The initial speakers all seem to be in the same place, probably the warehouse. They represent the Who's Who of organized crime on the East Coast. Then the voices seem to be projected from somewhere else. Having heard this once, it is a lot easier to follow. I am anxious to see the reaction by the assembled to the next few voices. "It is my pleasure to be with a group as dedicated as you are to the preservation of American values."

"Is that Congressman Hansen from Montana?" U.S. Attorney Feinstein literally jumps out of his seat. Billy pauses the CD.

"Please, be patient." Billy takes a step toward the ex-SEAL. Now that's a fight I'd love to see. Not really.

"Sorry."

Did I just hear Roger Feinstein being contrite? I glance around the room. Pete Spinelli has stopped pacing; Commander Marshall is awake...I think, and Captain Hancock looks terrible.

Billy restarts the CD player. If a congressman got Feinstein turned inside out, the next voice bounces him off the wall.

"I want to thank our hosts for putting together what I hope to be the first of a number of meetings. Getting this country back on track is my first responsibility, both professionally and personally."

"Christ almighty, that's Matthew Boyle!" Feinstein shouts.

"You mean the assistant deputy director of the FBI?" It looks like the State Police Commander is actually paying attention. Billy pauses the recording. So much for no interruptions.

"None other." Billy is really pleased with himself. "Captain...I assume that you can now appreciate my apprehension about the Bureau. Billy is more than willing to put up with these minor interruptions. He loves putting on a show.

"I've heard enough!" Captain Hancock rises, slamming the top of his desk. "Do you have any idea what you have?" He asks, pointing a finger at Billy. "Do you?"

"Yes sir, I know...and so do you."

"These are important people doing important things!" The Captain is shouting.

Both Feinstein and Spinelli are on their feet. I see Liz once again reach into her purse.

"Please Captain, sit down. This hurts me more than you can imagine." Billy's voice almost breaks with emotion. I knew this moment would come, but I wasn't sure how I would react.

"Sir, there may be a perfectly logical explanation. Before anyone says anything else, please let's finish listening to the recording," I plead.

Captain Hancock lowers his eyes, steps back and slides back into his chair. "Continue...Mr. O'Brien." His voice is like ice. Both Feinstein and Spinelli remain standing.

"Gentlemen, please sit down." Billy is clearly in charge.

The introductions continue. The voices are clear and recognizable. We hear them on the TV every day. Captains of industry and finance, those who influence policy, proudly greet the other participants. Current and former power brokers, as well as those whose names are probably unknown outside their neighborhoods, all exchange salutations. Some are in e-attendance and some are physically in the warehouse. The audio is far better than I would have expected and there is no mistaking Captain Hancock's voice. When I heard him earlier in the car, I felt as if my world had imploded. The man I trusted... respected, how could he participate in a meeting with those he had sworn to protect us from? I control the urge to stand up and scream. I sense Billy feels the same. He pauses the recording.

"Captain, please, please explain," I beg. "Tell me how you could associate yourself with people who believe they are above the law? I...we need to know." My voice comes from deep within.

"I thought the answer is obvious. The only law we have is the law from above. God's law...not man's law. Look at what has happened to this country — illegal aliens taking jobs from Americans, inter-racial marriages diluting the gene pool, gays in the military threatening our values. We even have a black president. We are becoming a second-class nation. Those men..." the Captain points a shaking finger at the CD player, "...are the real heroes. They are willing to fight for America. To die for America. We need to be strong. We need to be pure. Just...just look around." Captain Hancock lets his face fall into his hands. No one is dry-eyed. How could he become so twisted?

"Billy, did you have any idea?" I ask.

"About the Captain, not until I saw him arrive at the meeting. He always seemed like the perfect cop. I became a little concerned because I think he saw me standing next to some other drivers. He probably had me followed from then on. Remember, when I was apprehended? Boston's finest arrived at the shooting scene within a minute after I entered the building. Come on, Skippy...Chris, gun shots in Dorchester don't usually get that much attention. And putting you as the investigating officer was a great move. Didn't it occur to you that everything was a little too perfect?"

"Billy, I never suspected a set-up. The Captain personally asked me to take charge and I did. Never gave it a second thought."

All of a sudden, the Captain bolts out of his seat. The leather chair crashes to the floor behind him. He's got our full attention. Everyone is standing. Liz makes no attempt to restore order.

"None of you understand. Just wait. Maybe not in your life-time but in the life-time of your children and grandchildren, we will become a nation of mutts."

What happens next is surreal. The Captain reaches under his desk, presumably to ring for James. Instead, he brandishes a single shot Derringer and before any of us reacts, he places the tiny gun to his head and pulls the trigger. There is only a little pop, but the result is clearly effective. The Captain's body seems to be suspended in the air, but only for an instant, as his lifeless form crumples to the floor, bleeding into an Oriental carpet. We are all paralyzed, although I guess if Liz, Billy and I are really honest, this is the ending we expected. And maybe it is for the best.

Pete pulls out his cell phone and dials 911.

CHAPTER FORTY-TWO

Everything is happening way too fast. I can't get my arms around the fact that within 48 hours everything in my life has changed: I was able to put closure on my divorce; I met a woman who I might be in love with; reunited with my best friend and lost the closest person to a father I had. There was so much I wanted to say to Captain Hancock and standing at his gravesite doesn't seem like the right time. I feel that we have all somehow been cheated. Sudden death does that, but it is worse when the death is self-inflicted.

Funerals have always freaked me out. I guess it goes back to when I was five and my grandmother died. It was an open casket service at St. Johns in North Cambridge. I couldn't understand why my grammy wouldn't wake up and talk to me — she looked so much at peace. I don't hold to the belief that death is a beginning. To me, it is an end — permanent and forever.

If there is anything comforting about the Captain's funeral, it is that Trinity Church is filled to standing room capacity with people whose lives he touched in a positive way. Since there were five witnesses to the *tragic accidental shooting*, the press treats the Captain as a symbol of all that is good in law enforcement. I can live with that...I guess.

Needless to say, the casket is closed and a large blanket of gardenias is draped over the top. The entire sanctuary smells like springtime.

It takes almost a week to complete the forensic evaluation of the voices on the CD. Technology is amazing. We have gone from fingerprints, to DNA, to voiceprints and even retina prints. I get a painful twinge in my moral compass when I think that it won't be long before DNA samples are taken from each newborn in the country and stored for future use — whatever that use might be. George Orwell could never have imagined the extent to which Big Brother would be alive and well in the 21st century. I hadn't given much thought to the voiceprinting process until I watch it being applied to the CD. Each voice is isolated and printed. The print looks like the wave pattern you see on voice mail. In order to get a match you have to compare the unknown voiceprint with a known voiceprint. The FBI has a huge database of voices. Those that are assembled from the public speeches and interviews, and those that are assembled from wiretaps or other audio surveillance. There are tens of millions of voices already printed.

The harvest from Billy's efforts is bountiful. Over one hundred different people are identified. They come from every walk of life. Some are members of organized crime. Their participation I understand. Some are regular people, like Captain Hancock. Their participation I do not understand. I am both gladdened, as a former cop, and saddened, as an American citizen. Intellectually, I understand what the Captain was saying, but nothing can rationalize holding yourself above the law.

To defend their actions, domestic extremists cite Thomas Jefferson's now infamous letter to William S. Smith, which he wrote in 1787: "God forbid we should ever be twenty years without such a rebellion. The people cannot be all, and always, well informed. The part which is wrong will be discontented, in proportion to the importance of the facts they misconceive. If they remain quiet under such misconceptions, it is lethargy, the forerunner of death to the public liberty..." I believe this call to action has been taken out of context and is figurative not literal. Jefferson's world was too ordered to advocate for chaos.

I am reticent to share my thoughts with anyone, especially Liz, who seems preoccupied with work. I guess the payload generated by the recording has her attention 24/7.

After spending the week with Pete Spinelli, I understand why he felt limited in the Boston Police Department. The resources available to the CIA are extraordinary. For every voiceprint the FBI has, the Agency has a hundred or maybe a thousand. Every time anyone speaks publicly anywhere in the world, a print is made. Then the voiceprint is matched with fingerprints and whatever other identifiers are available including passport numbers, addresses, cell phones, Swiss bank accounts, mistresses' names and for those unlucky Americans on the CIA watch list, social security numbers. If the Agency's database ever fell into the wrong hands, the resulting identity theft would probably bring the world's economy to a screeching halt.

I am not sure what my current role is in this investigation, but everyone seems to consider me an insider. I'm glad I've got something to do to take my mind off...things. Going to the gym no longer has the same interest as before. I miss Liz. "Chris, I've got to go to..." He clears his throat. "...Eastern Europe." Pete's announcement snaps me out of my daydream. "The latest challenge that requires my attention is petro terrorism. I'm only surprised that it took this long to be a major threat. The price of gas changes the risk-reward ratio. *Pax vobiscum*...and thanks."

"And with you," I reply automatically. "I'm glad that everything worked out for Billy. Thanks." Pete had somehow secured a pardon for all of Billy's transgressions and even offered him an embassy posting.

CHAPTER FORTY-THREE

I am beginning to appreciate Roger Feinstein. Not that I like him, or that I would like to watch a Red Sox game with him, but his work ethic is infectious. He literally attacks the voice data that has been assembled. He wants to know everything about everybody who is on the CD. It's like a military operation, which is not surprising. While the Captain's death has affected us all in different ways, surprisingly, the ex-SEAL continues to be very bothered. At first I attribute this uncharacteristic expression of sensitive emotion to the fact that his career is about to be launched into the stratosphere. Being appointed the chief prosecutor of the guest list assures that his professional future is secure. Maybe a judicial appointment, assuming that the party affiliation of those who are prosecuted doesn't make it look like a reward for bringing down political leaders based upon partisanship. However, the recording is so graphic and the conduct so egregious that anyone caught up in this web will get little sympathy...maybe.

As much as I still think Feinstein is a bit full of himself, he shows compassion and guts when he forces the government to keep Captain Hancock out of the entire prosecutorial process.

I am about to leave the FBI offices in the John Joseph Moakley Building for what I hope to be the last time, when Roger, my new best friend, well almost, approaches and tells me that his father, a Holocaust survivor, felt that America was drifting in the wrong direction. Mr. Feinstein senior would yell at the phone whenever he heard 'press two for Spanish'. "I came to this country speaking no English. In two years I could do the New York Times crossword puzzle...in pen no less. Learn the language or leave the country." He extends his hand, which I accept.

"Chris, have you ever considered joining the Bureau? Not a desk job, but not front line, more as a strategy analyst. You've got the best instincts about situations and people that I have ever seen, except about me. I am really a nice guy." He smiles.

"Thanks, but no thanks. I've decided to either become a trout fishing guide for Orvis or a commentator for Monday Night Football, but I am undecided." I let go of his hand. "Good luck."

"You, too."

What probably doesn't come as a surprise to some, Commander Marshall announces his retirement. It's been a busy week. He writes a glowing letter of commendation for Detective Elizabeth Browne, citing her selflessness, bravery, intuition and professionalism and recommends that she be promoted to Captain. But that's another story. From the moment we met, Marshall was an enigma; he was a senior officer in a well-respected branch of law enforcement, but didn't seem to be connected. I suspect that there was something else going on in his life. I'm glad for Liz, I guess.

I am forever grateful that I don't have Billy's job; listening to the recordings over and over again. Many of the participants, whose voices were not in the database, were identified by good old police work, performed by none other than William O'Brien. Some of the voices he was able to identify from having worked for them, but others required attaching the voice to a name he had heard. The U.S. Attorney's office then requests the Court give them permission to wiretap to get a comparison print. Unfortunately, we don't have much time to talk. There was a lot I want to say. We decide to meet at the Irish Rose in South Boston for a pint...or two.

Billy enjoys being back in the neighborhood. He has received more than his fair share of ink for his role in what is being called the largest single assault on domestic terrorism. Although there are plenty of folks in Southie who share some of the beliefs of the far right, they are prepared to work within the political structure to make changes. Voter turnout in Irish precincts is consistently the highest in Boston. Also, the percentage of Irish in law enforcement in Boston far exceeds that of any other ethnic group, so that the revelation that Billy was working for the CIA, rather than the Mob, makes him a bit of a celebrity.

The Rose would be full 24 hours a day if they weren't forced to close at 1 am and not open until 8 am. Although it seems a bit early for a drink, the hours of operation are suited for a working class neighborhood. There is a place to wet your whistle when your shift is over. Service is fast and the room is noisy. Kind of like home.

"So now what?" I ask.

"Skippy, I need a change of scenery. I've been running solo for too long. Billy needs to take care of Billy."

"There is a certain irony to all this that I can't reconcile."

"I know," he says. "I think the Captain knew that he was putting it all on the line. And I think he knew how it would play out." Billy takes a sip of beer.

"But why us?" I ask.

"I think that he considered us unwavering. Willing to sacrifice everything for what we believed."

"Just like he did." I shiver, although it's probably 80 inside the crowded pub.

"And he knew that we would be the ones."

"I guess you're right, Billy, but I don't want to think that we caused his death."

"He caused it. We made it honorable. He was a good man. He always tried to maintain the image. Skippy, did you ever wonder why he never married? Captain Hancock was rich, smart, good-looking. Everything a woman should want."

"Wait a second Billy, you aren't implying —"

"I am implying nothing. I am saying that maybe the Captain wasn't able to reconcile certain things and therefore turned against those things."

"I still feel a lot of pain."

"Me too and probably a lot of others. The Captain was a great man. His limitation was his strength. Everything had to be as it should be. I think he felt the old ways slip sliding away and got swept up in the emotional tidal wave. Look at Nazi German. Hitler was able to create a fervor that resulted in good people ending up doing bad things."

"You are right but I wish he had reached out for help."

"The Captain was the one everyone else went to. No way could he reverse that and be the one seeking help."

"Billy, you've become quite the philosopher."

"I've seen more than my share of this planet and those who inhabit it."

"To his memory!" I raise my mug. He clicks his glass.

"To his generosity!" Billy toasts.

I can't quite believe that the Captain left both Billy and me $500,000, especially because of everything. Maybe he knew and he wanted it to end that way. Maybe he got in over his head and was trapped and the only way out was death. These thoughts should make me feel better — maybe a little.

"I knew the Captain was well off, but never did I imagine that he was a benefactor of so many charities."

"Think about it. He never spent what he inherited. Took home a very good paycheck and lived modestly. The brownstone was paid for. He didn't even own a car. He never traveled. James and his wife lived at Joy Street and I'll bet the Captain had to force them to accept any money from him."

"So where do you want to go?" I intentionally change the subject.

"At first...anywhere. Remember, I was reasonably sure that after the news broke there would be a contract out on me. A lot of Family members are going down. Call it the luck of the Irish, it turns out that there was a feud brewing between several factions within the Family and a very significant segment of the older Dons didn't think making deals with Spics and Chinks was good business. I eliminated the problem without a single shot being fired and suddenly, I'm a hero."

I raise my mug. "To the luck of the Irish."

CHAPTER FORTY-FOUR

Two weeks to the day after the Captain first called me, my phone rings.

"Callahan."

"Hi, stranger."

"Not by my choice."

"Chris, there's been a lot happening."

"You could have picked up the phone."

"I needed a few days."

"Try a few weeks."

"Sorry. Kiss and make up?"

It's pretty hard to pass up an invitation like that, even with a bruised ego. Well, it's really only been a week. "Sure...where and when?"

"Can I talk to you later?"

I can feel the old Dear John coming. "No problem. I think I am going to hook up with Billy later anyway."

"Did he finally decide where he wants to go?"

"He is going to England. He has interviews at Cambridge for their graduate program in Classics. He hopes to start classes next term. He may go to Greece to stand in the footsteps of Plato and Socrates."

"Are you going with him or just meeting him for a beer

and a burger in Southie?"

"Depends."

"On what?"

"I'm not sure. I got to go. Someone is ringing my doorbell. Call whenever." I think I may have shot myself in the foot with Detective, soon to be Captain Browne, but it doesn't look like there was much momentum. Funny, I think that Captain Hancock's death hit Liz pretty hard. You know, traveling in Europe with Billy wouldn't be a bad idea. The doorbell rings again. Who would possibly visit me in the middle of the afternoon? I hope I didn't leave any broken hearts at the gym. Which reminds me, I had better get back into my routine. The bell rings again.

"Coming," I yell. I open the door.

"It took you long enough."

"You said you were going to call later."

"No, I said I want to talk to you later. This is later."

My heart begins to race. Liz looks great. Light gray cashmere turtleneck sweater, simple strand of pearls, charcoal wool pants and UGGs. Can't have everything. Most importantly, she is carrying her leather overnight bag.

Also by D.G. Stern

Hot Tea…Cold Case
A Stephen Blackman Mystery

For younger readers:
Upton Charles - Dog Detective:
Disappearing Diamonds
Something Fishy
Winter Wonderland

Non-fiction:
GOLF a la CARTE-Volume One

NEPTUNE PRESS

WWW.NEPTUNEPRESS.ORG